Anastasia

The Last Grand Duchess, Russia, 1914

Carolyn Meyer

SCHOLASTIC INC.

Copyright © 2000 by Carolyn Meyer

ISBN 978-0-545-53578-6

12 11 10 9 8 7 6 5 4 3 2 1   13 14 15 16 17 18/0

Printed in the U.S.A.   40
This edition first printing, November 2013

The display type was set in Aphrodite Text.
The text type was set in Adobe Caslon Pro.
Book design by Natalie C. Sousa
This edition's photo research by Amla Sanghvi

For Patricia Clark Smith

Russia
1914

The Dowager Empress Marie Feodorovna Romanov

REQUESTS THE PLEASURE OF YOUR COMPANY
AT A WINTER BALL
IN HONOUR OF HER GRANDDAUGHTERS

The Grand Duchess Olga Nicholaievna

The Grand Duchess Tatiana Nicholaievna

The Grand Duchess Marie Nicholaievna

The Grand Duchess Anastasia Nicholaievna

ANITCHKOV PALACE, ST. PETERSBURG
ON THURSDAY, THE SECOND OF JANUARY
ONE THOUSAND NINE HUNDRED AND FOURTEEN
AT EIGHT O'CLOCK IN THE EVENING

DANCING AND SUPPER

3 January 1914
Tsarskoe Selo

Well, that's over, and I'm glad of it. I hate dancing. I'd rather climb trees any day! My feet still hurt — especially the toe that clumsy Lieutenant Boris stepped on while he was trying to waltz. What an oaf.

Hundreds of people attended the ball — all the court society of St. Petersburg, Papa says. If you piled all their jewels in a heap, they would weigh at least a ton.

Mama had a headache and left before midnight. Our little brother, Alexei, is feverish again, and Mama wanted to be at home with him. I wish I could have gone with her, but that would have upset Grandmother. She is already annoyed at Mama, I think.

Grandmother gave us each a diary as a keepsake of the ball. Olga and Tatiana and Mashka (that's what we call our Marie) have begun pasting things in theirs — the invitation, the menu for the midnight supper, the program of music played by the orchestra, and my sisters' dance cards signed by the officers who danced with them. (I did <u>not</u> collect my dancing partners' signatures.)

It was very late when Papa had the sleigh drive us from Anitchkov Palace to board our train for the ride back to Tsarskoe Selo. He sipped tea while my sisters chattered all the way home. I could hardly keep my eyes open but pretended to be wide awake.

4 January 1914
Ts. S.

I've decided to write a play about the ball. I'm calling it *The OTMA Snow Ball: A Jest in One Act.*

OTMA is the name we made up with the initials of our first names — Olga, Tatiana, Marie, and Anastasia. That's me, trailing along at the end, the youngest, the last of the Romanov sisters. Papa calls me *Shvibzik*: "Imp."

When I told my sisters about my play, Mashka said, "What a good idea! We can perform it for Mama."

Olga added with that worried look of hers, "Promise you will make it nice, Anastasia?"

I promised I would.

The Main Characters:

GRANDMOTHER — also known as the DOWAGER EMPRESS, wearing her diamond tiara and white brocade gown

PAPA — also known as NICHOLAS ALEXANDROVITCH ROMA- NOV, TSAR OF ALL THE RUSSIAS, in military dress uniform, with lots of ribbons and medals

THE GRAND DUCHESSES — OTMA

OFFICERS from the yacht *Standart*

The Scene: Grand Ballroom of Anitchkov Palace (actually our library)

The Grand Duchesses enter. They are dressed in matching gowns of white silk embroidered all over with pearls and crystal beads, and satin slippers.

My slippers pinched, but at least I didn't have to wear a corset. This is because I don't have a "figure," as Olga calls it. She's eighteen and has one. So does Tatiana, who's sixteen, and Mashka, who's fourteen. I'm twelve and haven't yet gotten a bosom. When I say "bosom," my sisters are shocked.

"Say 'figure,' Anastasia," Olga corrects me. "Proper ladies don't speak of . . . of bosoms." She blushes when she says it.

"But I'm not a proper lady," I remind her. "I'm a *shvibzik.*"

7 January 1914

Well, we did it. Mama's friend Anya Vyrubova came to our rooms after supper. And we rounded up Dr. Botkin and his son, Gleb, and Baroness Buxhoeveden and as many of Mama's ladies-in-waiting and Papa's gentlemen as could be found to make up the audience. There was no one to play the role of the Dowager Empress, of course, and so we put one of Mama's tiaras on an embroidered cushion on a gilt chair and pretended <u>that</u> was Grandmother.

Papa put on his white dress hat with a gold braid. First he bowed to Olga, and she curtsied, and then they danced while he whistled a waltz. Papa is the best whistler! Next it was Tatiana's turn, and then Mashka's.

I would have been next, but I decided not to play myself in this production. Instead, I borrowed a pair of tall black boots and a white jacket from one of the servants and took the role of Lieutenant Boris. Shura, my nurse-governess, painted a huge black mustache on my lip. Alexei made me a cocked hat of folded paper. Then I ordered my sisters to dance with me while I pretended to stomp all over their feet. (Mashka said I didn't pretend <u>enough</u>, and that I really did step on hers. But it was truly not on purpose.)

It ended badly, because Alexei insisted that <u>he</u> was going to dance "like Lieutenant Boris," and he got rowdy and crashed into Mama's table. Now we're afraid he'll get one of those terrible bruises and be ill again.

9 January 1914

Faugh! I detest schoolwork! Monsieur Gilliard, our French tutor, says that my efforts "lack inspiration." What he means is, I am lazy. We've been working on the pluperfect tense, and what could be inspirational about that? I was supposed to write my sentences ten times each, but I "forgot" a few of them and instead drew a border of flowers around the paper. M. Gilliard says that my flowers don't make up for lack of inspiration.

10 January 1914

Just as I feared, Alexei is in bed again, his knee swollen up like a cabbage and paining him horribly. When Alexei is not well, our whole family suffers with him. We take turns sitting by his bed and reading to him.

The servants tiptoe in and out, asking in whispers, "How is the tsarevitch?" And Mama always gives the report, "He seems a little better today, thanks be to God." Or, "He needs our prayers. Don't forget him!"

Of course everyone in the palace prays for Alexei, because he is the tsarevitch, the son of the tsar, and will be the next tsar of Russia, after Papa. No one must know that he's so ill. "It would alarm the people," Mama and Papa tell us.

Alexei is a bleeder. That means he suffers from a disease called hemophilia. (I probably didn't spell that right. Mr. Gibbes, my English tutor, complains that I'm a dreadful speller.) However it's spelled, it means that if my brother hurts himself, there's no way to stop the bleeding. A small cut on the skin isn't so bad. But if he injures a joint, or if something happens to make him bleed inside his body, then the blood is trapped. His joint swells up and hurts him, and he cries awfully. Then Mama turns pale and presses her lips together and begs us all to pray.

There is no cure for this disease, and nobody knows what to do, not Dr. Botkin, who checks all of us every day for signs of rashes and sore throats and such, nor Dr. Derevenko, Alexei's special doctor.

The only one who can help Alexei is Father Grigory, the holy man who is Mama's friend. Mama sent a message to Father Grigory to come.

Later

Alexei is much better. He always gets better when Father Grigory prays over him.

11 January 1914

A sunny day, but so cold, it makes my teeth hurt. Just as we finished our morning lessons, Papa came out of his study, where he had been working since breakfast, and announced that we must go ice-skating. My sisters and I dressed in our warmest woolen skirts and thick stockings and fur jackets and ran outside with Papa. Alexei couldn't go, but he waved to us from his window on the second floor in the south wing of the palace.

We ran to the lake in the middle of the imperial park, where the servants built a roaring fire near the warming hut. As soon as we'd strapped on our skates, Papa got us playing crack-the-whip. I challenged Mashka to a race and won. I couldn't beat Tatiana, because she's the tallest and her legs longest, but when I grow more I'll beat her with no trouble.

Papa stopped us often to make sure our noses were not getting frostbitten. "Keep moving! Keep moving, my dears!" he called out, but we didn't need this advice, because to stand still in such weather is to freeze solid as an ice statue.

Later Mashka asked if I remembered the time I made a snowball with a rock inside and threw it at her, and it knocked her almost unconscious.

That was wicked of her to mention it. Of course I remember! Olga Alexandrovna, Papa's younger sister, scolded me that day until I cried. Papa never scolds me, and Mama hardly ever. It's only Aunt Olga who does. Yet she's my godmother, and I love her best, after Mama and Papa! But nobody in this dratted family will let me forget that stupid snowball.

12 January 1914

Dr. Derevenko just finished examining Alexei and says he is improving, but cautions that he mustn't be allowed to run about and do dangerous things. Alexei loves to do dangerous things! So do I, but I'm not a bleeder. Girls are not — just boys, who inherit it from their mothers. I once overheard Shura gossiping about it: It was Mama's grandmother, Queen Victoria of England, who passed it on through her daughters' blood to their sons and grandsons. I wonder if I shall pass it on to my sons? <u>Not</u> something I can ask Mama.

14 January 1914

Alexei is much better, and we're all relieved. Whenever he is ill, life seems to hang suspended, as though we have all stopped breathing. Then, when he's recovered, we start living again.

It was Father Grigory who cured Alexei this time, Mama's sure of it. Gleb Botkin says that his father and Dr. Derevenko positively <u>detest</u> Father Grigory. They're convinced that he's a fraud. They even say that because he's a *moujik*, a peasant, he has no official family name, and that people in his village in Siberia call him Rasputin. (It's an ugly name meaning "dissolute," that he has no morals.)

Mama would be very upset if she knew how much the doctors dislike Father Grigory, because she believes in him absolutely. So does Anya Vyrubova — she introduced him to Mama a long time ago when she heard about his miracles of curing the sick and hoped that he could help Alexei.

And so we must all believe in him, even if he looks very strange. He is tall and strongly built; his hair is parted in the middle, long and dirty; and his beard is long and dirty as well. Mama says this is a sign of his humility, that he cares nothing for things of this world. When he looks at you with those fierce blue eyes, it's like he's staring straight into your soul. It makes me shudder! He seems not to bathe much (he does smell rather awful — like Vanka, Alexei's pet donkey — but of course I can't say that to <u>anyone</u>).

15 January 1914

I wonder if my sisters are writing in their diaries every day. Mashka scarcely bothers, I know that much. She's at least as lazy as I am (maybe worse). Papa and Mama think it's important for us to keep diaries. And Mama says we should also be using both Old Style and New Style dates, as she does. This is because Russia uses the Julian calendar, and most other places in the world use the new Gregorian calendar, which is thirteen days <u>ahead</u> of ours. For instance, today is 15 January in Russia, but in England and Germany and lots of other places, it's already 28 January. How strange! And what a bother! But if Mama says we must, then we must. I'll start tomorrow.

This morning I crept into the Big Pair's room (Papa calls O and T "the Big Pair"; M and A are "the Little Pair"), but I saw no diaries lying about. They must have hidden them. I thought of asking, but realized the question was fat-witted. They would certainly not tell me!

So I've decided I must find where each one is kept. I'll take a look from time to time, just to make sure they're actually writing in them. I'm going to search for Olga's first, because she's the oldest and most likely to have interesting secrets — although what they could be, I can hardly imagine. We already know everything about each other.

16/29 January 1914

(Ugh! I suppose I'll get used to this eventually.)

How we do love our evening baths! Until a few years ago, when Olga begged Mama to intervene, we took cold baths every morning because Papa believes they're good for you. He has one every day as soon as he gets up, just as he has done since he was a boy. Fortunately, Mama took our side and convinced him that young ladies do not need to be brought up like soldiers. And so now we have the luxury of warm baths in our big silver tub before we retire.

But that's the end of Papa's indulgence. The four of us sleep on camp cots. We must rise before sunup and make up our beds under the stern eyes of our maids, who tolerate no laxness, such as lumpy bedcovers. Then we join Papa for breakfast. I should love to have chocolate and pastries, but no! It must be rye bread and herring, or it's not "a good Russian breakfast" in Papa's eyes!

When Papa disappears into his study to work — he has much to do as the autocrat of All the Russias — my sisters and I go to Mama's boudoir, her private sitting room. She lies among the pillows on her chaise longue and helps us decide how we should dress for the day, always in matching outfits.

At precisely nine o'clock we march off to our classrooms and devote ourselves to French with M. Gilliard, to English with Mr. Gibbes, and to Russian with Professor Petrov. And all that other nonsense about mathematics and geography. Botheration!

18/31 January 1914

I have found Tatiana's diary! She puts it under her pillow. I would never leave mine in such an obvious place. I keep it in my wardrobe, beneath a pile of chemises.

Got up at 7 A.M. Had breakfast with Papa. Went to Mama, who suggested the navy blue and white outfits for today: something cheerful, to remind us that spring will come eventually. A. looks so funny in hers — like a little barrel.

I'm "A.," obviously. I do <u>not</u> look like a barrel in the blue and white outfit, and it's stinking of her to say so! But I do admit that it's not as elegant on me as on her, just because I'm still short.

19 January/1 February 1914

More from T's diary. She goes on about how much she enjoys her class with Monsieur Gilliard, because she "loves the sound of the French language." What balderdash!

Mama and Papa insist that we must learn all these languages, as they did when they were young. "When I first came to Russia to marry your papa, I had to study very hard to learn Russian." Poor Mama — she still blushes whenever she tries to speak Russian, but we are careful not to tease her. Papa speaks Russian to us and English to Mama. Mama speaks English to us, and sometimes German, which we are also supposed to be learning.

Mama was born in Hesse-Darmstadt, part of Germany, but she says she is completely Russian in her heart and soul, and she wants no association with Germany — especially not with her cousin Wilhelm, who is the kaiser of Germany, as Papa is the tsar of Russia. (Cousin Willy's country is tiny, though, compared with Russia. <u>Everything</u> is tiny compared with Russia.) Mama says she doesn't trust Willy.

Later

I've gone through T's diary, and every single entry sounds the same as the one before.

Exercise out of doors with Papa at eleven, even though bitter cold. Lunch at twelve with Mama and Papa. Practice piano for one hour. Tea at five, same as always.

And so on. No wonder she doesn't bother to hide her diary: It's <u>very</u> dull.

21 January/3 February 1914

Ha! Olga thinks she is so clever! I found her diary disguised as a book of devotions — imagine that! She covered it with a jacket of black leather and put it on her shelf with her other prayer books. Her diary is slightly more interesting than Tatiana's. For instance, last week she wrote this disturbing entry:

Poor Papa! He seems so weary these days — as though he carries a tremendous weight on his shoulders. Something is troubling him deeply.

What can it be? I'll have to pay closer attention.

23 January/5 February 1914

Tatiana is right. Tea is exactly the same every day, always the same boring bread and butter and biscuits.

Mama says that when she was a young girl spending her summers in England with her grandmother Queen Victoria, the teas were much more interesting than ours. All sorts of little sandwiches and cakes! But Mama can do nothing about it, because teas are always done the same way in the imperial family. That's us.

So, at exactly five o'clock, Papa walks into the library and butters himself one slice of bread, which he eats while he drinks two glasses of tea. (We have our tea the Russian way: The samovar keeps the water hot, and the tea is served in tall glasses set in silver holders. Mama says that in England, tea is served in lovely porcelain cups with saucers.) Papa reads his newspaper, and when he's finished he goes back to his study, where lots of serious-looking men wait to see him.

It must be difficult to be the most important man in the world — more important than any king, and certainly more important than Mama's cousin Kaiser Willy.

Later

Papa <u>does</u> seem distracted, and I think I know why.

Papa loves Russia and the Russian people more than anything in the world, and most of them worship him. Last year, to mark the three hundredth anniversary of the Romanov reign, our family took a boat trip on the Volga River. The idea was to retrace the journey of the first Romanov tsar from his home in the town of Kostroma to Moscow. As we were passing through a small village, I saw an old man fall down and kiss my father's shadow, because even the shadow of the tsar is holy.

But Papa has explained to us that not everyone adores him. Not everyone believes that he is the Father of Russia, and that Mama is the Mother of Russia, even though she loves the Russians as much as he does. There are people who say the peasants are suffering, and blame it on Papa. There are even some people who believe that others should share in the rule of our country!

That's nonsense, of course. Only the tsar must rule. Now it's Papa. Someday, years and years from now, it will be my brother, Alexei, the tsarevitch. This is God's will, so how could it be any other way?

I think it's because he believes some people don't love him enough that Papa looks so sad.

24 January/6 February 1914

I'm writing this in Mama's boudoir, next to the bedroom where she and Papa sleep. I'm supposed to be practicing French, but writing in my diary is more interesting — or *plus intéressant*, as they say.

This is Mama's special place. Everything is mauve — mauve walls, mauve silk curtains, the chaise longue covered in mauve satin.

M. Gilliard says that lots of the words we use are French — this is his attempt to persuade me that there's some point to studying his favorite language. For instance, *boudoir* is French (pronounced boo-DWAHR), and it means, "a place to sulk." I wonder if Mama knows that? And then *mauve* (pronounced MOHV) is also a French word for that pale bluish purple color that Mama adores. And *chaise longue* (pronounced shez LOHNG) means "long chair."

So there: I've done a French lesson without even being told. My reply to all of it is *Pfui!*, which is German for "Faugh." M. Gilliard should be proud of me.

Later

Twenty-nine degrees of frost, but we went outside, anyway. I nearly froze my fingers taking pictures of Alexei being pulled on his sled by Vanka, his donkey, and of my sisters. They refused to pose because of the cold, so it's just whatever I could catch them doing.

26 January/8 February 1914

Tomorrow we are going to a wedding in St. Petersburg, and today my sisters talk about nothing but gowns, jewels, hair, slippers, furs, and who will be there. The bride is my cousin Irina. Her mother is Papa's sister, Xenia. Irina is very nice, but she has six younger brothers who are the worst creatures in the world. The two oldest, Andrew and Theodore, are fairly civilized, but the rest are terrors. Nikita, who's a year older than I am, once accused me of biting him. This is definitely not true, because I would never get that close to him.

28 January/10 February 1914

What a splendid wedding! Irina was a beautiful bride, and everybody was talking about her lace veil, which once belonged to Marie Antoinette, Queen of France. Papa gave her in marriage — he's probably practicing for the four of us.

Irina's husband is Felix Yussoupov, who Papa says is heir to the largest fortune in Russia. As a wedding gift Papa gave them a bag of diamonds, which seemed strange to me because Felix probably already has all the diamonds he wants.

To my surprise, my cousins behaved like perfect gentlemen. But we left soon after the ceremony, because Mama wasn't feeling well. The boys may have been up to their usual tricks as soon as we were gone.

29 January/11 February 1914

The court photographer is coming next week to do our portraits, and Mama is in a dither about what we must wear.

Mama has had our maids carry dozens of our best dresses to her boudoir, where they're draped over every chair, and she changes her mind from one minute to the next. (The selections do not include that sailor outfit that Tatiana says makes me look like a little barrel. I shall <u>never</u> forgive her for that.)

I suggested peasant blouses, but Mama was appalled. That's one of her favorite words: <u>appalled</u>. I think she uses it about me more than about anybody else, except maybe when one of the servants does something wrong.

I don't think Papa was appalled in the least. I think he rather likes the idea. He often wears embroidered peasant shirts and soft boots, when he doesn't have to dress in a uniform weighted down with all those heavy medals and ribbons. If Papa is appalled by things I do, he never says so. He just smiles with those crinkly lines around his eyes and calls me *Shvibzik*.

Mama wants us to look like English princesses. The portrait of her grandmother, Queen Victoria, hangs in her boudoir. I often get the feeling that Queen Victoria is looking sternly at us Russian girls. She died before I was born, or I would probably have appalled her, too.

30 January/12 February 1914

Now I understand why Mama is having our portraits made. Yesterday I was casually leafing through Olga's diary (the one that looks like a prayer book), and I came upon this:

Papa says that Edward, Prince of Wales, is possibly interested in marriage. I told Papa that I am definitely not.

A suitable husband! For once I'm happy to be the youngest. I will not have to worry about such things as husbands and weddings for years and years. Poor Olga! Too bad it's a secret, because I would love to torment her about it.

———◆———

1/14 February 1914

Aunt Olga came out from St. Petersburg to spend the day with us, and we had an absolutely lovely time. After dinner Alexei insisted that she must visit his donkey. Vanka was hitched to a sled to pull Alexei, while we ladies rode in a sleigh. We stopped by the imperial zoo to say hello to the elephant that someone sent Alexei last year.

Then we all came back to the palace for tea. Tomorrow Aunt Olga is taking us to St. Petersburg.

2/15 February 1914
St. Petersburg

I love the city!

As always we went first to Anitchkov Palace for luncheon with Grandmother. The food was very elegant — not at all what we eat at home. Papa prefers what he calls peasant food, such as sauerkraut soup and *pirozhki*, little pies filled with rice and eggs. Mama doesn't eat much of anything and only nibbles at whatever is on her plate. But Grandmother loves French food! Today we had veal kidneys with wine sauce in little pastry shells. (I ate the shell and managed to hide the kidneys in my napkin.) Each of us had a footman to serve us. I tried hard to make my footman laugh, but he would not.

Grandmother presided at the head of the table, and each of us had to say something pleasant and polite, all while sitting up absolutely straight and using exactly the right fork and knife. When it was my turn to speak, I accidentally let out a belch. Even though I begged everyone's pardon, Grandmother was displeased.

At last we were excused, and we said good-bye to Grandmother and kissed her hand. (I love her perfume!) Then Aunt Olga whisked us off to her house.

She made us each lie down on a divan with our eyes closed for an hour before her guests were to arrive. I hate to lie down for rests! There's always too much to do. My sisters closed their eyes and are pretending to sleep, but Aunt Olga is allowing me to write in my diary instead.

3/16 February 1914
Ts. S.

I wish we had more days like yesterday!

After everyone had rested, our maids helped us dress — Mama had sent along our green velvet tea gowns with the white sashes and pearl buttons — and arrange our hair and fasten our jewelry.

As usual, Aunt Olga had invited the most amusing young people (including Lieutenant Boris, the one who stepped on my feet, but he's not so bad when he's not dancing). After we had tea with some nice little cakes, we played charades, which I adore, because I'm really quite clever at acting out the parts. And then this same Lieutenant Boris produced a harmonica and began to play a lively tune. Soon we were all calling out songs for him to play. That clumsy oaf of an officer turns out to be rather talented!

It was all over much too soon, and Baroness Buxhoeveden came to escort us back to Tsarskoe Selo. Now all I can think about is when we shall go to the city again.

If only Alexei would stay healthy, and Papa not look so worried, and Mama smile a bit more, the world would be an absolutely perfect place.

4/17 February 1914

Father Grigory came to see Mama and Papa again. Such a strange man! He always comes to our rooms after we have put on our nightgowns and robes to say our prayers with us. I try not to get too close to him. I can't say exactly why I am so uneasy around him, aside from his eyes that stab like icicles. And his evil smell! I believe Mashka has noticed it, even if Tatiana and Olga pretend they haven't.

I don't think Shura likes him much, either. Once I heard her tell Dunyasha, Olga's maid, that she thinks it unsuitable for Father Grigory to visit our private rooms when we're not properly dressed for visitors. And Dunyasha promptly put Shura in her place, telling her that Father Grigory is this family's best friend, that Mama believes he was sent to her by God, and Shura has no business questioning that.

If this is so, couldn't God arrange for Father Grigory to bathe himself before he comes here? That's <u>my</u> question.

5/18 February 1914

When Dr. Botkin examined us this morning, he announced that I am coming down with a cold. I don't need Dr. Botkin to tell me that. We always knows when he's around, because of that French cologne he wears, but today my nose is so stuffed, I didn't even notice it!

Mama is afraid I'll have a red nose and look clownish in our portrait. If I cross my eyes, then I will look <u>truly</u> clownish.

6/19 February 1914

Thank goodness that's done! Mama finally settled on white dresses. Then there was a crisis of which jewels we should wear (first it was pearls, then sapphires, then pearls _and_ sapphires, and finally just pearls).

Anyway, Kremikov, the photographer, came with his great box and tripod. Every time he snapped the shutter and stopped to put in a new glass plate, the four maids would rush forward with brushes and combs and powder puffs. Extremely tedious. And Kremikov or Mama or one of the maids was always whispering loudly, "Anastasia, please be still!" Not an easy thing, with a dripping nose.

8/21 February 1914

The pictures I took of Alexei and my sisters are finished. Last evening we pasted photographs in our photo albums, with Papa supervising as usual. He is so fussy, the least little smudge of paste disturbs him. I always seem to have more smudges than all the rest put together.

The picture of Alexei and Vanka turned out best — Alexei's expression is quite imperial, and the old donkey, probably shivering under his thick gray hide, appears completely miserable.

I also took perfectly dreadful photographs of Olga and Mashka, in which Mashka looks fat and Olga looks stupid. I shall threaten to send them to their future husbands if they don't treat me nicely. No matter how I try to catch her off-guard, Tatiana never looks fat and stupid.

9/22 February 1914

Today is the first of Butterweek, a whole week of eating the richest, most delicious food before Lent begins. Once Lent starts, no meat, no milk, no butter, no cheese, and no eggs, for seven weeks. Even at teatime the menu will have one small change: Instead of a slice of buttered bread, Papa will have a small handful of nuts.

So for eight days there will be plates and plates of *blini*, little pancakes swimming in melted butter. I love them. I can eat more than anybody, and Tatiana says that if I put even one more in my mouth I will turn into a *blin*. That could prove interesting.

10/23 February 1914

Shura must have spoken to Papa about Father Grigory, because Papa told him that he must not come to our rooms at any time when we are not dressed to receive visitors. Then Father Grigory told Mama that he's going back to St. Petersburg and won't spend so much time here at Ts. S.

Now Mama is upset. I heard her tell Papa that Father Grigory is a true man of God who lives in poverty and offers himself as a guide to people who are suffering. Papa says that may be true, but that even a man of God must not give cause for talk. I agree.

Besides, Father Grigory no longer looks like a man in poverty. Mama made him a whole wardrobe of silk blouses that she embroidered herself, and he wears black velvet trousers tucked into leather boots as handsome as those Papa wears. Maybe someone will give him some bath soap.

13/26 February 1914

The photographer brought our portraits this afternoon, and I must say, they are very nice. We all look quite beautiful. You can't even tell my nose is dripping. My fear is that Edward the Welshman will see this and fall hopelessly in love with Olga and she will leave us.

—◦◦◦—

14/27 February 1914

Snow, snow, snow. The world is completely white. We've built a wonderful snow mountain for sledding. The servants helped us carry buckets of water to throw on it. The water froze instantly, and soon we had an icy hill to throw ourselves down at breakneck speed.

Mama doesn't come out in the snow with us the way Papa does, but in the afternoons she sometimes bundles up and goes for a drive in her sleigh with Baroness Buxhoeveden or Anya Vyrubova. They wear so many furs and bury themselves under so many rugs that all you can see are their bright eyes.

"Time for spring," Mama says with a sigh, and I know that she's already dreaming of Easter in the Crimea.

16 February/1 March 1914

Aunt Olga came yesterday and took me to St. Petersburg for the day. Since the weather was fine, we rode in her open carriage, accompanied by several of the palace guards on horseback. We drove along Nevsky Prospect, a beautiful boulevard bustling with automobiles and trolley cars alongside elegant carriages. We passed shops with displays of dresses and hats and jewelry in the windows, and a glass-roofed shopping arcade as big as a cathedral.

Girls my age were strolling past the shops with their mothers or aunts, chatting and pausing to look in the windows. I pleaded with Aunt Olga to stop.

But she shook her head, explaining that grand duchesses do not go into shops. When I asked her why not, she said, "Because it isn't done." And then she told me not to annoy her with so many questions.

17 February/2 March 1914

Last evening we put on a musicale for our parents and all the usual — Anya, the countess, Dr. Botkin, M. Gilliard. It's maddening that Tatiana practices the least and still plays best of the four of us. She swept through her Tchaikovsky as though the palace were on fire. And Mashka played the "Moonlight Sonata" very well, and Olga played "Claire de Lune," a modern piece by the French composer Debussy.

Then there was my Chopin. I've been working on the preludes for weeks and thought I was making progress, but my fingers turn thick and clumsy the minute I have an audience. When I finished, I announced that the Polish composer would have been pleased to know that his piece could be played by ten Russian sausages. (Mama was <u>appalled</u>, as usual.)

Alexei had a surprise for us. He's been taking lessons on the *balalaika*, a traditional Russian stringed instrument shaped like a triangle. He played "Kalinka," one of Papa's favorites. Papa jumped up and began to dance to it, and we had a terrific time.

Later

The Great Fast began today. My stomach has been growling since early morning. Mama suggested that I spend time in prayer to take my mind off my stomach. And then I got a lecture.

Mama reminded me that before she married Papa and became Russian, she was a Lutheran. She said she wasn't sure she could marry Papa, because that meant giving up her Protestant faith and becoming Russian Orthodox. Yet she believed that she was meant to be Papa's wife. So she prayed and prayed, until at last God spoke to her, and she understood that she could best serve Him as an Orthodox believer.

Mama says that fasting is good for the soul. (She must have an excellent soul, because she eats hardly anything, anyway.) I'm not like Mama. Neither is Mashka, whose lips are still shiny with yesterday's blini. And I'm still hungry.

19 February/4 March 1914

Something very funny happened today. Mama usually rests all morning in her boudoir, reading and writing, with Eira, her shaggy little Scottish terrier, at her feet. Then the maids help her dress in her gown and jewels. Tatiana goes to comb her hair. Mama has beautiful hair, and no one can arrange it as well as Tatiana. Alexei and Mama lunch together, and we four sisters join our father and his guests for a formal luncheon.

But today Eira somehow got loose and went racing down the hall, chased by all six of Mama's wardrobe maids. She managed to get as far as the dining room just as Papa arrived with his aides and some visitors. Father Vasilev, our family priest, who always blesses the noon meal, was coming in the opposite direction. Eira took one look at the old priest with his black beard drooping down to his waist, and began yapping madly. Father Vasilev began flapping the huge sleeves of his long black robe and shouting at the dog to go away. He looked like a giant crow. That made Eira even more frantic.

I started laughing, but finally one of Papa's secretaries managed to catch the dog and take her back to Mama. Mama just adores that silly dog. Most people can't stand the animal.

Father Vasilev composed himself and shouted out his blessing of the food in his old, cracked voice, just as he always does. And our luncheon proceeded as though nothing at all had happened.

21 February/6 March 1914

The wind is howling with such force that even Papa decided not to go out into the teeth of the storm.

Instead, when lessons were finished this morning, Mama allowed me to come to her boudoir to paint. She says I'm like my aunt Olga in my talent with pens and brushes. It's very cozy here. Everywhere you look are vases filled with flowers from the greenhouses in the imperial park.

When they were first married, Mama and Papa lived with Grandmother in St. Petersburg. Later, they moved here to Tsarskoe Selo, which means "the tsar's village." There are two palaces, and we live in the smaller one, the Alexander Palace. It has over one hundred rooms. (The Catherine Palace, which I can see from Mama's window, has more than two hundred.) I haven't even been in them all. In one wing of Alexander are the apartments of all Mama's ladies-in-waiting, like Baroness Buxhoeveden, and Papa's suite of aides, and other people who help us, like Alexei's doctors.

In the center section are the official rooms where Papa receives important visitors. The halls are very long — I once tried roller-skating in one of them, but they are made of marble, and my skates made such a clatter that people came rushing out to see what was going on. From every ceiling hang enormous chandeliers that must be cleaned, one little crystal at a time. It takes a lot of people to keep the chandeliers sparkling!

Our rooms are in a separate wing, which Mama has fixed up nicely, like an English cottage, she says. Here in her boudoir the walls are covered with icons, beautiful Russian paintings of religious figures, and the portrait of Queen Victoria looking very stern — not at all like our grandmother, the dowager empress, who is very gay and witty.

24 February/9 March 1914

Papa says that when he was a boy Alexei's age, he was instructed to keep a diary. And he has written in it every single day since!

I promised myself that I will write in my diary every single day, but this is hard because there isn't much to write. My diary is every bit as dull as Olga's. Every day is the same: get up, make my bed, eat breakfast with Papa, visit Mama, study with our tutors, go outside with Papa, eat lunch, practice the piano, more study, have tea. I want something <u>exciting</u> to happen!

26 February/11 March 1914

In two weeks we leave for Livadia, our palace in the Crimea overlooking the Black Sea. Now <u>that</u> will be a change! Mama is eager to get away from the extreme cold, and so are we all. The maids have begun pulling out our spring outfits and packing them in trunks, and our tutors remind us daily that even though we're traveling to warmer climes, our lessons will continue, regardless!

M. Gilliard reminded us that Papa will continue working, just as if he were here in Tsarskoe Selo. He was looking directly at me when he said it.

7/20 March 1914

One of our door attendants, Jim, asked me to take a photograph of him in his uniform: scarlet trousers, a black vest embroidered in gold, and a white turban. This is the costume worn by the Ethiopians whose duty is to open and close our doors whenever someone goes in or out. Jim is going home to America for a vacation. (He is not really Ethiopian, but he is very tall, and black, like the other door attendants.)

I took the photograph and promised him several prints to take with him. He thanked me and said his mother is proud that her only son has such an important position. I think it must be dreadfully boring to stand there all day waiting for a chance to open the door, but Jim says he likes to see all the interesting people who come and go. And it makes him feel "big" to work for the most powerful man in Russia and probably in all of Europe and maybe in the whole world. But Jim says Papa is no more important than Mr. Woodrow Wilson, who is the president of the United States, elected by the people.

He explained how Americans choose someone to rule for four years at a time. It seems silly to do it that way, but I didn't want to argue with Jim.

9/22 March 1914

Father Grigory came to give us a special blessing and to wish us a safe journey. Mama brightens up when he's here, because he reassures her that all will be well.

He stayed to dinner with us. His table manners are appalling. If I ever behaved so, Mama would certainly scold me. But because he is a man of God, he is forgiven his manners — scratching himself, even picking his nose! I know I ought not to have done it, but when I saw him, I began to pick mine, too. Mama didn't notice, but Tatiana shot me a murderous look, and Mashka kicked me under the table. No one shot a murderous look at Father Grigory and I'll bet nobody kicked him, either.

12/25 March 1914
On the train

Servants spent the night loading our trunks, and we left this morning in the middle of a snowstorm. Everyone was in a good mood.

The imperial train is like a palace on wheels. There are nine cars, painted dark blue and pulled by a great black locomotive. Papa and Mama have their own car with a bedroom and sitting room, in Mama's favorite mauve. Papa has his study with a big desk and leather chairs in another car. My sisters and I have a bedroom for ourselves — no camp cots, but real beds! And Alexei shares his room with Derevenko (not the dear doctor or his son Nikolai but one of the sailors who always watches over my brother).

The bathtub is the most cunning thing: It's specially built so that when the train goes around a curve, the water doesn't slosh out. All the ladies-in-waiting and Papa's aides have their own compartments, and the servants have theirs. My sisters and I eat at the long, narrow table in the dining car with our papa and the other guests, and Mama usually takes her little meals with Alexei.

15/28 March 1914

Here is something curious: A <u>second</u> imperial train that looks exactly like this one is a few miles behind us. Alexei got the bright idea that he could have that one all for himself, and really his question was quite sensible: Why should all of us be on this train when there is another perfectly good train?

I could see that Mama didn't want to answer Alexei's question. Finally Baroness Buxhoeveden, who is very blunt and plainspoken, explained to Alexei that the second train is a decoy, to confuse would-be assassins, so they won't know which train to blow up.

"I see," said Alexei gravely. But he didn't, because later I heard him ask Papa the same question.

Papa explained it this way: Powerful people are often disliked. The tsar, like all powerful men, has enemies, and it's possible that someone might try to harm him. So as a precaution, there are two trains. But Papa told Alexei that he wouldn't like to travel in the other one, because the food is not nearly so delicious.

16/29 March 1914

We're crossing the steppes of Ukraine, a huge area far to the south of Tsarskoe Selo and St. Petersburg. Outside the windows of the train I can see the beginnings of spring. The train moves slowly, about the speed of a galloping horse, but it won't be long now until we cross into the Crimea.

Papa has been making this long journey to the Crimea since he was a young boy, with Grandmother and Grandfather and Papa's brothers and sisters. Grandmother has told us stories about the old days, when Grandfather was still alive. Tsar Alexander III was "big as a bear and twice as gruff," she always says, sounding proud. One day in the fall of 1888, the entire family was aboard when, suddenly, the train came off the rails and the cars tumbled over. The roof of the car in which they were riding was completely caved in. Imagine how frightened everyone must have been!

But Grandfather was so strong that he pushed up the roof of the car and held it while everyone crawled out.

It's hard for me to picture my grandfather, who was more than six feet tall and very surly at times. My dear papa is not like that at all. He is just five feet seven inches tall but very handsome, and he is the kindest papa and the kindest tsar in the whole world. That's why I don't understand why anyone could ever be angry at him.

18/31 March 1914
Livadia Palace

Here at last! It's so sunny that the light hurts our eyes. All around are steep cliffs, little Tatar villages tucked in the mountainside, gleaming white mosques, and the sparkling Black Sea. (It's not black at all. I don't know why they call it that.)

Livadia is Mama's favorite palace because she and Papa built it just a few years ago. Everything is new and lovely and bright, and we have beautiful views of the beach and the sea.

In November of 1911, soon after the palace was finished, Mama and Papa celebrated Olga's sixteenth birthday here with a grand ball. She dressed in a pale pink gown, with the necklace of diamonds and pearls they had given her (the rest of us were in white). She wore her hair up for the first time and looked very grown up and beautiful. I told her she looked fat and ugly as mud, but instead of getting angry, which she should have, she hugged me and said that Papa and Mama will do the same for each of us as we come of age to be presented. (I don't want to be presented. It sounds like what our chef does when he brings the Easter lamb to the table.)

When the dancing ended at midnight and a buffet supper was being served, the moon rose and reflected on the sea below us in a silvery pool. It was so lovely. I was sorry I told Olga she was ugly as mud, for she is not.

———•———

19 March/1 April 1914

It's still too cold to swim in the sea (Papa doesn't think so; he goes in every day, regardless, always with a loud whoop when he hits the icy water), but we're to go for a horseback ride after our lessons tomorrow.

20 March/2 April 1914

My *derrière* hurts! Tatiana gets practically blue in the face when I say that word. It's almost as bad as <u>bosom</u>. I told her it's a French word and therefore perfectly proper, but she still disapproves. So I'll say it this way: That part of my anatomy that was in contact with the saddle of a horse for six hours is <u>sore</u>.

Even so, it was a good ride, back through the pine forests to a pretty waterfall. The farmers were plowing their fields for the spring planting, and they were very friendly. Papa says a swim in the sea would relieve my aches and pains. Mama says a warm bath is better.

———◆———

22 March/4 April 1914

Tennis lessons have begun. Again. My tennis tutor says that I have a "natural swing," but swing as often as I do, I don't manage to hit the ball very often.

I would much rather watch Papa, who has a natural swing <u>and</u> hits it every time. He plays with some of his aides and others in his suite. Some of Mama's friends like to play, too, but Mama says her great joy is sitting quietly in the sun and watching the rest of us madly running after balls.

24 March/6 April 1914

Anybody would think we might have a few days off from our lessons while we are here in Livadia. But our tutors are merciless!

When Monsieur Gilliard and Professor Petrov at last dismissed us today, Papa took us for a very long walk. We met some Turkish-speaking Tatar women who dye their hair with henna and hide their faces behind long veils. I think someday I'll dye my hair bright red and wear a veil and no one will know who I am. Won't Mama be appalled!

27 March/9 April 1914

I found Mashka's diary. I <u>swear</u> I wasn't even looking for it — it was simply lying there, open, on her table. Naturally, I looked. Here's what she wrote:

Someday, when I am grown up, I shall marry a Russian soldier and have twenty children.

She must be crazy.

29 March/11 April 1914

Papa's sister, Aunt Xenia, and her husband, Uncle Sandro, have arrived with our cousins. Irina is still on her honeymoon with Felix, but all six boys are here. Alexei is beside himself with happiness to have some boys to play with, but Mama doesn't like them any more than I do, because they're rowdy. I plan to stay as far away from them as possible, <u>especially</u> Nikita.

30 March/12 April 1914
Palm Sunday

Today begins the holiest week of the year. Mama spends a great deal of time in her little chapel praying before her dozens of icons, holy pictures of the Virgin Mary and Jesus and the saints. Sometimes Papa or — more often — Tatiana goes with her. I usually manage to be somewhere else when she's looking for one of us to accompany her.

31 March/13 April 1914

I'm decorating eggs to give to my family. First, you make a tiny hole in each end of the egg and blow <u>very hard</u>. (The chef takes the blown-out insides to make cakes for the Easter feast. He doesn't believe in waste.) I don't want to mention how many eggs I squashed until I had an entire row of empty eggshells to decorate. I've finished two: The first is dyed deep red with bits of gold-colored straw glued on in an intricate pattern. That one is for Papa. The other is dyed mauve, painted with purple irises, and shellacked, for Mama.

1/14 April 1914

We had our last fitting today with the seamstresses making our Easter dresses. They're silk in a misty kind of green that Mama calls *celadon*.

She says we'll look extremely sophisticated when we wear them to church on Easter Eve. I say "Faugh!" to <u>sophistication</u>, but not out loud in front of Mama.

3/16 April 1914

Shura had to help me with my sisters' and Alexei's eggs to get them finished in time. I used one of the leftover eggshells to make a false nose, which I wore to tea to see if anyone would notice. Papa pretended not to, but Mashka laughed, Alexei shrieked, and — imagine! — Mama was appalled!

Easter Day 1914

Last night, the sophisticated Romanov grand duchesses and all of Papa's and Mama's guests crowded into the silent, darkened church. At midnight, the bishop knocked loudly on the door of the church and shouted, "Christ is risen!"

and the crowd roared back, "He is truly risen!" The bishop entered carrying three huge candles, from which the priests lit their candles and passed the flame to ours, until hundreds of candles flickered. Mama's face glowed with joy, and so did my sisters', but I was having trouble with my garters and expected my stockings to fall down around my ankles. So, the only glow from me was my red face.

After the service we came back for a wonderful feast. Lent is over, so we can eat all those things we weren't allowed for the past forty days. The best is the *paskha*, sweetened cottage cheese mixed with candied fruits and nuts, then baked in a mold shaped like a flowerpot. I told Olga I could eat *paskha* every day, and she said that if I did I would soon <u>look</u> like *paskha* (like a flowerpot, she means). She is rotten, and to get back at her, I told her I know she secretly tried some of Dunyasha's rouge on her lips. She grew quite red in the face, so I know she probably had. Mama does not allow <u>anyone</u> to wear rouge.

Later

Everyone was here for Easter dinner. Another feast! Butter, molded in the shape of a lamb, sat in the center of the table. It's the dearest thing! There were platters of cold veal and wild boar and so on, and of course *kulich*, the most delicate bread. Yesterday, I watched the chef lay the loaf on its side on a pillow to cool so that it doesn't get flat or out of shape, because it's as tender as a cloud. The chef carried our *kulich* to church last night to have it blessed.

The food was delicious, but the guests were not, at least not all of them — our dreadful cousins, for example. Mama invited Mrs. Phelps, that English lady who wears hats that look like a nest of birds. She has a voice like a bird, too. After Mrs. Phelps fluttered off, I did a little imitation of her, cawing exactly the way she does. Papa and my sisters were laughing so hard that tears were rolling down their cheeks, but Mama said my manners were frightful.

Papa said, "That's our *Shvibzik*." And winked at me.

As usual, Papa presented Mama with the most glorious Easter gift: a jeweled egg. I'll describe it tomorrow. Now I'm going for more *kulich* and *paskha*.

7/20 April 1914

Long ago, Grandfather began the custom of ordering a jeweled egg every year from the court jeweler, Carl Fabergé, as an Easter gift for Grandmother. Now Papa orders two eggs, one for Grandmother and one for Mama. This egg is much bigger than an ordinary hen's egg, or the egg of any other kind of bird (why am I now thinking of Mrs. Phelps?), and is made of gold and lots of precious jewels.

There's always a surprise inside the egg that's revealed when you push a secret button. For instance, it might be a basket of wildflowers made of pearls. We each have a favorite egg: Tatiana loves the one that has miniature portraits of her and Olga and Papa inside. I love the one with a little crowing cock that pops out of the egg. Alexei likes the one called the Great Siberian Railway Easter Egg. Inside it is a tiny exact model of the Siberian Express, made for Easter in 1900, the year the railway was finished.

Papa leaves the design of the eggs up to Fabergé, who always has to be careful that Mama's Easter egg is just as beautiful and clever as Grandmother's, and the other way around.

I absolutely love the egg Papa gave to Mama this year. It's called the Mosaic Egg. It's completely covered with tiny diamonds, emeralds, rubies, and sapphires that form intricate flower designs. The surprise inside is a cameo with the profiles of OTMA and Alexei carved on a pink stone that's mounted on a golden stand and surrounded by pearls.

We all admired it, but Alexei says his favorite is still the Siberian Express.

Papa put the egg I made for him in his study.

9/22 April 1914

Our cousins have gone! Thank goodness!

12/25 April 1914

Papa took us on another long walk. Mama and Alexei joined us later for a picnic, although Mama was feeling weak and needed her wheelchair. An odd thing happened. My sisters and I were picking wildflowers in a meadow, and Alexei was lying on a blanket nearby, staring up at the clear blue sky, when suddenly he said, "I wonder what's going to happen to us?"

We asked him what he meant, and he couldn't explain it — just that he had a strange feeling that something was going to happen, and that next year we wouldn't be here.

"Nonsense," Mama said, but I wasn't at all sure that he was speaking nonsense. Alexei has a way of sensing things.

17/30 April 1914

Edward the Welshman is not going to ask for Olga's hand after all! I don't know why — it can't have been because of the portrait — but I do know that Mama is annoyed. She wants Olga to go to England when she marries and leaves us.

Olga is relieved. She insists that she doesn't want to leave at all, and I don't want her to go.

19 April/2 May 1914

Of all the important people who come to visit Papa because he is the tsar of Russia, my favorite is the emir of Bokhara. He's the most fantastic-looking man — very tall and dark, with a long black robe, and a white turban that glitters with diamonds and rubies. The emir's mouth peeks out like a little red bird from the nest of his thick beard and mustache, not nicely trimmed like Papa's but lush as a raspberry thicket. He speaks to us in a droll manner and always brings us sweets and small carved animals from his country.

23 April/6 May 1914

Papa told a story at dinner today that had everyone laughing but me. Years ago, when I was only five, my sisters and I had gone swimming in the sea with Papa. Suddenly a great wave came along and swept me off my feet. The next thing I knew, I was being tumbled under the water, wanting to scream but not able to. I was sure I was drowning. Then I felt a yank on my hair. It was my dear papa, holding me by my long hair and towing me to the beach. But I thought it was Neptune taking me to his kingdom beneath the sea.

For the rest of that day I stayed by Mama and baby Alexei and refused to go back in the water. The next day Papa said I must come in with him. I did, and soon I forgot all about what had happened.

Today as I dashed into the water, Papa called out, "Watch out that Neptune doesn't grab you!" He loves to tease me.

28 April/11 May 1914

We have lots of birthdays coming up soon in our family. Papa's is next week, and then Mama's, and then Tatiana's. Mashka's is in June, after mine. We get such a tiny allowance, only twenty rubles each month, that it's hard to buy much. I bought Tatiana a pair of gloves recently when Madame Gheringer brought her cases of scarves and hosiery and other things for Mama to make her choices. I wanted to buy the white kidskin, but had enough only for lace. I plan to buy Mashka a bottle of her favorite scent, Lilas, when I've saved up some money.

Madame Gheringer is very thin, with a long, sharp nose and eyes set close together. I made a drawing of her in my sketchbook, but I dare not show it to Mama, who chastises me for mocking people.

2/15 May 1914

Another visitor: Mama's friend Lili Dehn. Lili's husband is first officer of Grandmother's yacht, *Polar Star*, and when he's at sea, she spends time with us.

Lili is very stylish — she loves the fashionable hobble skirts. When Lili explains that she wears them because they are the fashion, Mama frowns disapprovingly.

Papa's cousin, Grand Duke George Mikhailovitch, and his wife, Queen Marie of Greece, and their wretched children are here. Nina is the worst of the lot. She's exactly two days younger than I am but already a whole head taller! She thinks this gives her the right to lord it over me. I think she is putrid, and I told her so.

I can hardly wait for them to leave. I'm so much happier when it's just OTMA and Alexei. (So is Mama, I can tell.)

6/19 May 1914

Today is Papa's birthday. It's being celebrated very quietly. If we were back in Ts. S. there would probably be all sorts of ceremonies and reviews and such, and Papa would dress up in his uniform with all the gold braid and many ribbons and medals, and sit on his enormous horse.

We gathered in the courtyard for a lovely cake with lots of whipped cream. Mama has been keeping a sharp eye on Mashka and me, because she sees in us what she calls a "tendency to overweight." She does not see this tendency in Olga and Tatiana, who are both revoltingly tall and slim.

7/20 May 1914

It was Mama's notion that OTMA should entertain the friends who came to bring Papa birthday greetings. We were each to play a piano piece. I've made almost no progress on those dratted Chopin preludes. It's just that I do so hate to practice. As usual, my sisters performed beautifully. They've learned new pieces since our last musicale, and I have not even learned the old one well enough to satisfy either Mama or Miss Kropotkin, our piano teacher.

Grandmother didn't come for the event. She never comes here. I know I shouldn't say this, but I have a feeling that Grandmother and Mama don't like each other very much. They're always polite, of course, because it would upset Papa otherwise.

I believe it's because Grandmother loves parties and balls and such, and Mama doesn't. She just wants to be with her family. Sometimes I think Mama is very lonely, and she has only us for company. I even heard Aunt Olga say to Papa, when they didn't know I was present, "Surely, Nicky, you plan to have a grand ball to present Tatiana. She's nearly seventeen!"

And Papa said, "I don't think Sunny is quite ready for that yet." (That's Papa's name for Mama: Sunny.) He explained that Mama's nerves are quite strained because of Alexei's problem. That's how they always describe his illness: "Alexei's problem."

13/26 May 1914

Poor Olga! She is absolutely beside herself! Now Crown Prince Carol of Romania wants to marry her, and we are all going to meet the prince and his family. Olga dreads it.

Mama and Papa think that marrying Prince Carol would be a good thing for Olga. His mother, Queen Marie, is a cousin of both Papa and Mama. Since they are fond of this cousin, they believe that Olga will like Carol, who is twenty-one, just two years older than Olga.

I do my best to cheer her up, reminding her that Romania is right next door to Russia. But then I found a map and located Bucharest, the capital, and saw that it really is quite far from Ts. S. Still, I promised that we'd see one another often, whenever we're at Livadia.

And then I nearly wept, too, because seeing one another often is not like seeing one another every day.

16/29 May 1914

All anyone talks about is Olga's stupid rotten engagement. Our yacht, *Standart*, has come down from the Baltic Sea to take us over to Romania to meet King Ferdinand and Queen Marie and the crown prince.

Olga just sits in her room and sulks. She doesn't even want to talk to Mama, who is rather upset with her. Usually I'm the one Mama is upset with, so this is a nice change, although I do feel sorry for Olga.

19 May/1 June 1914
On the Standart

We love to be on our yacht, but not this time. We're en route to Romania. Olga's face is set in a grim expression. In a few hours we'll arrive in the port of Constanta, to be greeted by Prince Carol and his parents. This isn't the first time they've met: Carol and his family were all present at Olga's birthday ball in November two years ago. She says she danced with him twice, and that he's an acceptable dancer but strikes her as very silly. (I like silly people. Olga doesn't.)

20 May/2 June 1914
Standart; Constanta

King Ferdinand and Queen Marie must really want Olga to marry their son, because they put on a great show for us. From the minute the *Standart* entered the harbor while bands played and little boats shot plumes of water into the air, we had not a moment to rest. There was barely time to change clothes and get our hair fixed before we were off to the cathedral, a military review, a private luncheon, and a state banquet. It was too boring for words. The only thing even halfway fun was the fireworks that we watched from the deck of our ship. I thought the banquet would never end. Everyone spoke French.

I amused myself by trying to pick out the ugliest person at each gathering. This was very difficult, and kept me well occupied because there were so many possibilities to choose from!

Olga looked beautiful, as always, but very pale and very serious. I tried to make her smile by pulling faces at her, sticking out my tongue, crossing my eyes — everything I could think of. Nothing worked. Her face was like stone.

Prince Carol didn't have much to say, silly or otherwise. Afterward, we sisters argued about whether he was handsome or not. Mashka liked him, and so did Tatiana, but I voted against him because his hands were as clammy as fish. Olga voted against him, too, no surprise.

24 May/6 June 1914
Livadia

I had to search everywhere for Olga's diary to see what she's written about Prince Carol. (I found it hidden in the bathroom.) This is what I read:

I am a Russian and I will remain a Russian. I will never leave my country, even if it means that I do not marry.

I wonder what Mama will have to say to <u>that</u>!

When Olga makes up her mind to something, that's the end of it. Now I suppose Papa and Mama will have to find her a suitable Russian, although I can't think of any.

25 May/7 June 1914

Today is Mama's birthday. We had a quiet little family party, because she always says she doesn't want any fuss.

Tomorrow we leave for Tsarskoe Selo.

———————

26 May/8 June 1914
On the train

Farewell, Livadia! We're headed north again.

The train is dreadfully hot. Sometimes we stop in a shady grove to jump out and cool off. Olga mopes in her compartment. Alexei and I pass the time playing checkers. He said he thinks Mama will feel better when she sees Father Grigory again. That surprised me because I hadn't noticed she wasn't feeling well.

"Mama never feels <u>really</u> well, you know," he said, and calmly captured two of my men.

29 May/11 June 1914

This is Tatiana's seventeenth birthday. She likes her gloves — I'm sure she would tell me if she didn't. We played charades as the train rumbled along. Mama and Papa promised that she would have a grand ball in November when we go back to Livadia. But then I remembered what Alexei said, that we would not be back again, and it made me shiver.

30 May/12 June 1914
Ts. S.

The servants are always happy to see us when we've been gone for a while. Shura and our personal servants travel with us, but most of the others stay here unless they're sent to one of the other palaces. Jim, the Ethiopian from America, was one of the first to greet us. He brought me a jar of jam that his mother made for him. He says it's made with guava, a fruit that grows in America in what he calls "the South." I immediately sat down with a spoon and ate nearly all of it. I made myself half sick, but it was so delicious.

31 May/13 June 1914

Here's something interesting: Natasha, the daughter of our maid Dunyasha, is getting married. She came today to tell us about it. She is so excited — Vladya is a member of the Cossack guards. He's very handsome in his bright red tunic! The wedding is to take place next winter, and she's promised to tell us all her plans as she makes them.

Only Olga doesn't want to hear about it. She is out of sorts most of the time — "Grumpy," Mama says. She and

Mama seem to oppose each other quite often, and I'm sure it's because Olga refused to marry Crown Prince Carol and Mama says she ought to.

Tomorrow we're going to Peterhof, our summer palace by the sea.

1/14 June 1914
Peterhof

We call it "the farm" because this little palace is not as elegant as the one at Livadia (or the gold and white Great Palace nearby, which I can't recall us ever using). And the Baltic is very different from the Black Sea (<u>cold!</u>). But this is where I was born, and I love to celebrate my birthday here. Four more days and I'll be thirteen.

Maybe when I am thirteen my life will become exciting.

2/15 June 1914

What a splendid day! The British Royal Navy's First Battle Cruiser Squadron arrived on an official visit. This afternoon we were taken by launch to the admiral's flagship, *Lion*, and given a tour by the midshipmen. They are so handsome! Even Olga was smiling.

Three more days.

4/17 June 1914

Tomorrow is <u>the day</u>, my birthday, the day that everything will change. If I keep saying that, I'm sure it will.

Mama's cousin Kaiser Wilhelm sent me a doll from Germany for my birthday. A doll! I am so disgusted. It's true that it's beautiful, porcelain with blue eyes like Mashka's, and she's dressed most elegantly with a little rabbit fur jacket for winter, but <u>still</u>! Doesn't that idiotic Cousin Willy understand that I am no longer a <u>child</u>?

5/18 June 1914 - My birthday

(If I write two dates, shouldn't I have two birthdays?)

I'm up early, waiting for something to happen.

Here's a story that no one in my family knows that I know. I heard it from a servant named Lutka.

It's the custom that when the tsar and the tsaritsa have a baby, a salute is fired: 300 rounds for a boy, and 101 rounds for a girl. The reason, of course, is that a boy will be the next tsar, and a girl will be only a grand duchess. Anyway, when Olga was born — according to Lutka, who was there — the gun was fired 101 times. The next time it was Tatiana, who was greeted with only 101 rounds. The third time Mama was waiting for a baby, Mashka appeared. <u>Boom</u>, 101 times.

Then, when Mama was expecting her fourth baby, the churches were filled with people praying for a tsarevitch. Candles were lit, and the priests said special Masses. No one prayed harder than Mama!

And out popped another girl — <u>me</u>! No one had to tell me that an awful lot of people were disappointed when a fourth grand duchess was squalling in the nursery!

But here's what Lutka said: "Your papa cried! I saw him with my own eyes, weeping at your birth, Anastasia! They were not tears of joy, believe me! But then he collected himself and went into the tsaritsa's bedroom with a smile on his face just for her."

I don't know if that part of the story is true or not. Lutka is no longer one of our maids. I didn't even have a chance to say good-bye to her when she left.

When I was three years old, Alexei was born, and the Russians at last heard three hundred rounds for the tsarevitch. He was — and still is — the most important child in Russia.

6/19 June 1914

<u>Nothing</u> happened. Nothing <u>exciting</u> happened. Maybe my exciting life will begin very gradually.

We did have a nice party—Aunt Olga and Anya Vyrubova came, and Dr. Botkin and Gleb. All the usual people. And the usual gift from Mama and Papa: another diamond. They give me a diamond or a pearl on every birthday and name day so that when I am sixteen I shall have a beautiful necklace with thirty-two beautiful gems, just like my sisters'.

As a special treat, Aunt Olga and I went for a walk with our easels and my new watercolors and sat under a tree and painted. When we came back to the palace for tea, there were special tiny cakes that Grandmother's pastry chef made especially for me and sent along with Aunt Olga. Anya ate so many, I thought she would explode. But she did not. She resembles a little sofa, soft and puffy, all dressed up in a flowered slipcover and toddling along on pudgy feet.

Tatiana says I am not a good one to talk, because I'm getting fatter, too. She actually said such a mean thing on my birthday.

8/21 June 1914

Grandmother invited my sisters and me to lunch at Anitchkov Palace in honor of my birthday and Tatiana's, and Mashka's next week. As usual we had a French menu (*escargots en beurre* — snails in butter — ugh!) and spoke only French throughout the meal. Her gift to me was a silver music box that plays a pretty tune and has a ballerina on top, who dances when I wind it up. I did remember to say *Merci beaucoup*, which is French for "Thank you very much," and I kissed her three times, Russian style.

Then she promised to take me to Paris. (At least that's what I <u>think</u> she said; my French is far from perfect.)

I asked her when — in French, of course — and she said, "For your sixteenth birthday, Anastasia Nicholaievna."

But that's not for three whole years! How can I bear to wait that long? (She didn't say if all four of us are going. Mashka will be sixteen next year, and Grandmother didn't say a word about taking <u>her</u> to Paris, but she's too good-natured to be jealous.)

———◆———

11/24 June 1914
On the _Standart_

Our small yacht took us from Peterhof this morning out to the _Standart_, which was waiting for us in deeper water. The brass band was playing as we boarded, which put us in a merry mood. Mama and Anya immediately found their favorite white wicker chairs on the deck, and we began our summer cruise in the Gulf of Finland.

I love to watch the white plumes of smoke that pour out of the white funnels. Papa says the _Standart_ is 128 meters long and more splendid than anyone else's yacht — more than Grandmother's _Polar Star_, more than Kaiser Wilhelm's _Hohenzollern_. (Papa says Cousin Willy is horribly envious of ours.)

Every night before dinner, Papa, the men in his suite, and the ship's officers gather in the lounge for _zakuski_, little appetizers like pickled reindeer tongue, and radishes carved into flower shapes, and dark bread with roses made of butter. The men stand around eating and drinking and talking. Then we all go in to dinner together. The officers are so dashing in their sparkling white uniforms. I think Tatiana has been flirting with a tall, redheaded second officer named Saltikov.

12/25 June 1914

Last evening at sunset when the ship's guns were fired (I have no idea <u>why</u> they do this every evening), I stuck my fingers in my ears and let my tongue loll out of my mouth, as though the sound of the cannon had done me in. Mama <u>hates</u> it when I do this. She says I am unladylike, and that such behavior is appalling.

After that little bit of nonsense, Mashka and I took a stroll around the deck. She went to our cabin to get a wrap, but I wasn't at all cold, and continued to wander around by myself. That's when I saw Tatiana flirting quite madly with Officer Saltikov.

She saw me watching her and demanded to know what I was doing, "skulking about and spying."

I said I wasn't skulking <u>or</u> spying, I was simply strolling in the moonlight. Later, when Tatiana came to our cabin, Mashka and I both accused her of flirting outrageously (even though Mashka hadn't actually seen her and had to take my word for it). Tatiana denied everything, but she did blush the rosiest color!

I told her that if she could accuse me of skulking and spying, then I could accuse her of flirting. She had no answer to that.

Later

Why couldn't everything go on being perfect? Alexei
has had an accident. He jumped from the ladder when
we went ashore this morning, and fell and twisted his
ankle. Now that dreadful disease has flared up again,
and he is in horrible pain. Mama is quite beside herself.
She blames Derevenko and Nagorny, the two sailors
who are constantly with Alexei, for not watching him
closely.

Since he was five years old it has been their job to make
sure he doesn't hurt himself. Not an easy job for anyone,
especially since Alexei is determined to do everything any
other boy can do. Mama always tries to protect him, but
Papa wants him to grow up to be as strong as possible so
that he can be a good tsar.

14/27 June 1914
On the Standart

We had a lovely birthday party for Mashka, with music and
dancing and lots of food. Mama and Papa gave her the most
beautiful sapphire that's the exact color of her eyes. We like

to tease her about her eyes, so big and round that Papa calls them "Mashka's saucers."

Now she's fifteen, and she has already begun talking about "when I am married" and "when I have little ones." She's probably dreaming of her Russian soldier and their twenty children.

15/28 June 1914

Alexei was well enough today that Papa decided the rest of us could go hiking. Tatiana stayed on the yacht with Mama and Anya because Mama always likes to have one of us around. (I think Tatiana agreed so she could flirt with her officer.)

Early this morning the launch delivered Papa and Olga and Mashka and me to a little island, where we spent the day picking berries. Mashka accused me of eating more berries than I put in the basket, but that is absolutely untrue.

When we got back to the yacht, Mama was in the lounge, playing piano duets with Anya. Mashka brought her a bunch of wildflowers, and I made up a story about a bear chasing us in the berry patch and acted it out for her, taking the part of the bear.

"There was no bear, Anastasia," Tatiana said. And when I

asked how she knew, since she wasn't there, she said she was watching the whole time through the telescope.

16/29 June 1914

Bad news came over the wireless at noon today: Archduke Franz Ferdinand of Austria-Hungry was assassinated yesterday. He was riding in an automobile in Sarajevo when a crazy man shot him and his wife. Papa knew the archduke. He says he was a friend of Cousin Willy's.

At dinner tonight, everyone was talking about the assassination. The officers usually want to flirt with us (with my older sisters, and sometimes with me), but there was no flirting this evening. The brass band plays marches in the evenings, but Papa asked them for something else. Instead, they played Tchaikovsky's *1812 Overture*. At the end we had some fireworks, which Alexei loves. Alexei's leg still hurts him, but he's very brave.

17/30 June 1914

Much worse news today. Someone attacked Father Grigory with a knife and tried to kill him. He was badly wounded, but all of us are praying for his recovery.

Mama is terribly upset, and Anya weeps inconsolably. "Such a good man! Such a man of God!" she cries, over and over, and wonders who could ever wish him harm.

Mama says it was arranged by one of his religious enemies. Even a man of God has enemies!

18 June/1 July 1914

Alexei was the first to sight the *Polar Star*, Grandmother's yacht. Our two yachts dropped anchor side by side, and Grandmother was brought from hers to ours in a small boat and then lifted on board with a special chair.

We had tea on the deck — the sun was hot, but the white canvas shades were up, so no one got scorched — and then OTMA presented the little skit called *The Bear*. I've been working on it for days. Alexei played the part of the bear, carried on the shoulders of Derevenko. We found a great brown rug to drape over both of them, so the bear looked quite fearsome. Tatiana and Olga were maidens in need of rescue, and I was the hunter who almost shot the bear.

Before she went back to the *Polar Star*, Grandmother asked Papa what he had heard about the archduke's murder, and he told her what he knew: that the assassin was a Serbian, and that Cousin Willy blames it all on the Serbian government.

"Watch out for Kaiser Wilhelm," Grandmother said. "He's such a bully, you know."

I don't think she said a word about the awful thing that happened to Father Grigory, because she doesn't like him at all. I can tell by the way she twists her mouth whenever he's mentioned. This is another reason why Mama and Grandmother aren't fond of each other.

20 June/3 July 1914

This morning on our hike with Papa, I collected a whole pocketful of pretty rocks from the beach and brought them back for Mama. They seemed to cheer her up a little. After lunch Papa went to his study (he works two days a week when we're on our cruise), and my sisters and I roller-skated on the deck. I can skate faster than Mashka, who's always afraid she's going to crash into something. I never think about crashing.

23 June/6 July 1914

A thunderstorm broke this afternoon, and the sea was wild and churning. We stayed in the lounge, where Mama played the piano for us while spray lashed the windows.

The music she always plays is sad, and when I begged her to play something cheerful, she just looked at me and said, "But, my darling, life is sad."

I know that she was thinking of Father Grigory. We pray for him every morning, and at night, too.

26 June/9 July 1914

Papa seems determined not to let his worries spoil our yachting holiday. Today we went ashore to hunt mushrooms. (Mashka stayed with Mama.) Papa built a little fire and pulled out a pan and some butter from the pack he carries. He cooked the mushrooms, and we ate them with bread.

Later I got in trouble with Tatiana. Olga went off by herself to read, and Papa went for a swim. He left his cigarettes on the beach. I took one and lit it and was holding it between my fingers the way Papa does and only pretending to smoke it. Suddenly Tatiana leaped out of the bushes and threatened to tell Mama. I tried to explain that I was playacting.

Tatiana said it looked an awful lot as though I had actually been smoking, and I reminded her that I had seen her holding hands with the redhaired officer and it looked an awful lot as though she had kissed him. So I don't think she'll tell Mama, but, anyway, I'm not touching Papa's ciga-rettes <u>ever again</u>.

30 June/13 July 1914

Today was so fine that we persuaded Mama to come ashore with us for a picnic. Tatiana's redhaired officer carried Mama and helped her get settled on a rug. Then he spent most of his time gazing cow-eyed at Tatiana, and Mama had to ask him twice to bring her parasol.

No mention of cigarettes or smoking.

This evening we're having a dance. I wish Mama would allow me to wear my hair up, but I know she won't.

3/16 July 1914

Last night was so much fun! The balalaika orchestra played for dancing, and we all got to choose our partners. Olga, who didn't even want to dance and said she'd stay in her cabin and read, ended up coming to the dance after all. And she chose the redheaded officer as her first partner! Naturally Tatiana couldn't say a word and had to ask someone else. I could hardly keep from laughing.

I picked Papa. He says I dance very enthusiastically.

6/19 July 1914
Peterhof

Today our cruise ended, and we're back at the farm. Mama and Anya are in a better mood because Mama has a letter from Father Grigory. He's in his village in Siberia recovering from his wounds, but he writes that he's feeling strong again.

Not everyone is happy. Olga is glum, and Tatiana was sorry to see her officer sail away. Actually he hasn't gone far, because we'll continue to take short cruises.

I searched everywhere I could think of for her diary, to see if she wrote anything about kissing him, but the dratted girl has hidden it very well. I <u>still</u> think she kissed him.

15/28 July 1914

More news that has everyone worried. The Austrians have attacked Belgrade, the capital of Serbia, to get even with the Serbians for what happened to the archduke. Papa spends lots of time in meetings with his advisers, trying to decide what to do. The Serbians are our allies, and we have promised to help them if they are attacked. That means there might be a war, and we must get ready for it.

16/29 July 1914

Papa sent a message to his generals ordering our Russian soldiers to prepare for war. He is so brave and looks so anxious — the pouches under his eyes are bigger than ever. Papa and Cousin Willy could actually end up fighting against each other if there is a war. Papa showed us on a map: Because Russia must help Serbia fight Austria-Hungary, Germany would side with Austria against us. Then France and Great Britain, who are our allies, would fight on our side against Germany.

We all pray for a miracle to stop the war, because Papa says many men will lose their lives when the fighting begins. Now we're waiting to see what Cousin Willy, the kaiser of Germany, will do.

19 July/1 August 1914

What a terrible day! I shall never forget it.

Papa stayed shut up in his study for hours with his advisers. When he finally appeared, he was as white as a ghost. "We are going to war," he said, leaning against the doorway. "Germany has declared war on Russia." Then we all began to weep, including poor, dear Papa, because we're so upset by the news and so frightened of what lies ahead.

20 July/2 August 1914
St. Petersburg

Yesterday is still kind of a jumble. We ate a hurried meal, changed our clothes, and left for St. Petersburg. Alexei had to stay in Peterhof because he can't walk, and Papa thought this was a bad time for people to see the tsarevitch in such a condition. So it was Papa and Mama and the four of us and our usual suite.

I had been feeling so sad and afraid, but it was quite thrilling to find the crowds outside the Winter Palace all cheering and singing. "Batiushka," they were shouting (that means "Father of Russia"), "lead us to victory!" And they sang, "God Save the Tsar" in a voice like a mighty roar.

The cheering went on and on. Dr. Botkin and Gleb were there, and Gleb kept going on about how great a thing this war was going to be for Russia. When I asked him if he wasn't frightened, he said, "The Germans don't know how to fight! They only know how to make sausages!" He says all we have to do to defeat them is throw our caps at them.

Dear Gleb, his excitement was so great that I began to feel excited, too. But one look at Papa's face tells me it may not be as easy as Gleb believes.

30 July/12 August 1914
Peterhof

This is Alexei's tenth birthday. Papa works constantly now, conferring with his generals about how to win the war, but he did take time to celebrate.

Of course everyone knows it's the tsarevitch's birthday, and so gifts have been arriving from people everywhere — except from Cousin Willy! Alexei's favorite is his new toy train, an exact replica of the Trans-Siberian Express. He also has several model boats for sailing on the lake.

Dressed in his sailor's uniform, Alexei relentlessly orders everyone around. My sisters and I always take care not to burden our servants, and we go to great pains not to give orders. Alexei doesn't believe in that at all! He is forever sending someone scurrying off to fetch him sweets. But it's understandable, because often he can't walk and must be carried around. I suppose I would be giving orders, too, if I had to sit still. Nagorny and Derevenko seem to take it in good humor.

1/14 August 1914

Papa says it's an ancient tradition to go to the Kremlin, the citadel in Moscow, to ask God's blessing on Holy Russia at the beginning of a war, so we're leaving for Moscow in a day or two.

4/17 August 1914
Moscow

The crowds that welcomed us here were even bigger and noisier than the ones in St. Petersburg. At least a million people jammed the streets and hung from balconies and tree branches for a look at us as our procession slowly moved along. Every church bell in the entire city was ringing and making a terrific din.

Poor Alexei is terribly upset, because he wants to appear beside Papa before the crowds, but he can't walk even a single step. Papa is determined that he'll appear tomorrow anyway.

———◆———

5/18 August 1914

Everybody is going absolutely wild, so happy to be Russian and so happy to have a tsar like Papa to lead us to victory. When we arrived here yesterday, Papa made an impressive speech at the Kremlin. We were all wearing our best dresses and hats and jewels, except Mama's sister Ella, who is the abbess of a convent here in Moscow and wore a plain gray habit. A Cossack soldier carried Alexei.

Then we all went to Assumption Cathedral, where Mama and Papa were crowned a long time ago, to pray before the icons and the tombs of important dead Russians. There was always much excitement and deep emotion.

I can hardly wait to see old Cousin Willy beaten!

9/22 August 1914
Ts. S.

We're happy to be back home, because a scary thing happened to Alexei while we were in Moscow. He and M. Gilliard decided to go for a drive in the country in a motorcar. But hundreds of people recognized the tsarevitch and tried to get close enough to touch him.

Finally some policemen rescued them from the jostling crowds, but Alexei was terrified, and Mama was angry at M. Gilliard for sneaking off like that.

13/26 August 1914

Papa has made a big decision: He's changing the name of St. Petersburg, which sounds German, to Petrograd. It means the same thing in Russian.

Everyone is very patriotic, and no one more than Papa. That's why the telegram from Father Grigory made him so angry. Father Grigory, who is still recovering from the assassin's attack, sent Papa a wire, which Anya delivered to him. I was there when Anya rushed into Mama's boudoir. "Father Grigory urged Nicky not to go to war," Anya cried. Then she said Papa was so angry, he tore the telegram into a dozen pieces.

Mama tried to calm Anya down until she could find out from Papa what was going on. Usually Papa and Mama agree with everything Father Grigory says, but not this time. Papa says Father Grigory has no business giving such advice and should stick to being a holy man.

23 August/5 September 1914
~~St. Petersburg~~ Petrograd

It's hard to remember that the name has been changed.

I was afraid I'd miss everything, being out at Tsarskoe Selo, because I heard from Gleb Botkin that every day here is filled with the sound of men marching off to war. But dear Aunt Olga proposed that OTMA should observe this stirring sight. She brought us into the city in her carriage so that we could witness the spectacle of our brave soldiers marching down Nevsky Prospect to the railway station, where they board trains headed for the front. There were lots of wives and children weeping and waving and cheering as their husbands and fathers went off to war. It was sad but thrilling.

24 August/6 September 1914

Luncheon at Grandmother's at Gatchina Palace. She forbade all talk about the war and instead turned her bright eyes in my direction and asked me to tell her about my study of French poetry.

That was a disaster, of course. But after luncheon, when we went back to Aunt Olga's, it was a different story. All the young men talked of nothing but the war. Lieutenant Boris plans to take his dress uniform with him when he leaves for the front, so he'll be ready for the victorious parade through the streets of Berlin. No one seems to give the least thought that he might get wounded or even killed. They expect to be home by Christmas.

28 August/10 September 1914
Ts. S.

Papa left this morning for *Stavka*, the headquarters of the army. He's going there to consult with Grandfather's cousin, Grand Duke Nicholas Nicholaievitch, the commander-in-chief of the armies. Papa says it's important to keep up the morale of the men with visits from the tsar, and also to make sure that all is going well. So far we have lost one big battle but won a bigger one.

30 August/12 September 1914

Mama has shocked us all. Three weeks ago she ordered the Catherine Palace to be turned into a hospital for wounded soldiers, and now she's decided to become a Red Cross nurse! We're all amazed because Mama has never done this sort of work before, and her own health is never very good. Only a few weeks ago she had to be carried ashore from the *Standart* in a wheelchair, and now she's going to be a nurse!

1/14 September 1914

I'm spitting mad. Not only is Mama training to be a nurse, but so are Olga and Tatiana. But not Mashka and me. No! We are too young!

Mashka is so good, always so sweet about everything, and she has tried to make me feel better about being left out. "At least it's both of us, the Little Pair," she said, and then suggested that maybe we could find other good work to do for the soldiers. She's such an angel, I'm not sure we're truly sisters.

Mama says indeed we can be of great help, we can visit the sick and injured. But — we will not get to wear uniforms, and I did so much want to!

6/19 September 1914

Papa's home again. Things seem almost normal when he's here.

22 September/5 October 1914

Papa is back at *Stavka*, and we immediately started missing him horribly. Mashka and I went to Anya's for tea. She has such a sweet little house in the park near our palace. Father Grigory was there, completely recovered and dressed in a bright yellow silk shirt. He poured tea and talked about things that seemed to interest everyone but me. Anya hangs on every word he says.

27 September/10 October 1914

Our life here has turned completely upside down. We're not used to having Papa away so much, and Mama is becoming a different person. She used to lie in bed until noon, but now she's up every morning for seven o'clock Mass, breakfast at eight, and by nine o'clock she and Olga and Tatiana are dressed in their gray uniforms and white aprons with a red cross on the bib, and they're on their way to the hospital. And they're gone for the whole day!

Meanwhile Mashka and I stay here with our tutors, and Gilliard, Gibbes, and Petrov complain they have never seen such inattentive pupils as Mashka and Alexei and I. This is because we all are yearning to be somewhere else: Alexei at *Stavka* with Papa, and we two leftover sisters at the hospital with Mama.

Every time Mama finds one of her friends with an extra palace or mansion, she shames them into giving it to her for a hospital. She tells them, "You must do this for Holy Russia." Under her direction, eighty-five palaces have been made into hospitals for wounded soldiers and ten trains have been made into traveling emergency clinics.

Mama and the Big Pair are still in training. It will be another month until they are certified war nurses, but they are already in the thick of it. At teatime they come home filthy and exhausted, and they swallow their tea and gobble up their bread and biscuits before they have even bathed and dressed properly. Then they go on with their tales of terrible bloodshed and gore — fingers taken off because of poison in the blood; smashed bones;

awful-smelling wounds; men shot to bits who still hang on to life.

In the evenings after dinner, Mama writes pages to Papa, and so do my sisters.

I have nothing to write about to Papa except to tell him how much we love him and miss him.

30 September/13 October 1914

Anya brought Tatiana a little French bulldog. He's named Ortino. He is absolutely adorable! Mama's dog Eira hates him passionately.

My sisters play cards by the hour, but I find it dull. I'd rather paste pictures in my album to show Papa when he comes home.

7/20 October 1914

The only thing even faintly amusing these days is Ortino, who races around like a mad thing and sometimes leaves small piles of you-know-what on the carpet, so that we must always keep a little shovel handy. Such bad manners! (Even Eira is appalled!)

———◦•◦———

15/28 October 1914

Seven classes today! It's just too much. How do they expect me to keep all of this in my head? Professor Petrov is reading us a story by Turgenev, his favorite writer. He thinks I'm taking notes, but I'm really writing in my diary and will begin a letter to Papa if the professor doesn't catch me first!

Ortino has eaten one of Mama's shoes and is in disgrace — again.

30 October/12 November 1914

Mama, Olga, and Tatiana have completed their nurse's training. We're so proud of them! Mashka and I visit the wounded soldiers at Feodorovsky Gorodok, a small palace that Papa had built in the imperial park to resemble a traditional Russian village. It's been made into a small hospital. The soldiers are far from home and very lonely. Some can't even write their own names, poor things, peasants from the countryside who never learned their letters, and they ask us to write home to their mothers and sweethearts. We also read to them and feed those who are too weak to feed themselves. They're so grateful for every small thing we do.

3/16 November 1914

Olga's nineteenth birthday. She was too busy for even a tiny party.

5/18 November 1914

Mama is worried about her brother, our uncle Erni, the grand duke of Hesse, who lives in Germany and is an officer in the German army. They write to each other through their cousins in Sweden. People are saying awful things about the Germans, and some even say that because Mama was German, she must be awful, too. "All my heart is bound to this country," she says, and it doesn't matter where she was born. How dreadful people are.

8/21 November 1914
On the imperial train

We're on our way to *Stavka* to see Papa. He's back at head-quarters after a visit to the southern Caucasus to inspect our troops who are fighting the Turks. Anya came with us. She wouldn't miss a chance to see what *Stavka* is like.

10/23 November 1914
Stavka

Papa was delighted to see us and could not give us enough hugs and kisses. We're having a terrific time. Olga finally got a chance to celebrate her birthday. Nothing like last year!

Stavka is southwest of Petrograd on the Dnieper River, in the middle of a dense forest. Several army trains have been pulled up in the midst of the birch and pine trees, a roof put over them, and wooden sidewalks laid down. It's really quite cozy, like a little village.

At noon the motorcars drive us to a mansion in the town of Mogilev to have luncheon with the officers. I tease Mashka about finding a husband here.

"Don't be vile," she says, but she's blushing. She doesn't suspect I've read her diary and know she dreams of a soldier husband and twenty children.

It's grand to visit, but Papa seems even more worried than before. So many men have been killed, far more than anyone expected, and now it seems that the war won't be over by Christmas after all.

28 November/11 December 1914

Ts. S.

We are all outraged! The Holy Synod of the Church
has banned Christmas trees because they're originally
a German custom. Mama has written to Papa about it.
She says it's narrow-minded to outlaw something that
brings so much pleasure to children and to the wounded
men in the hospital. But Anya says there's not much she
and Papa can do, because so many people call Mama
Nemka, "the German woman," and believe she's a traitor. This makes me terrifically angry, but there's nothing
I can do.

20 December 1914/2 January 1915

Aunt Olga came today and told us that the windows of
German bakeries in Petrograd have been smashed. I
remember how I wanted to go into a dear little candy shop
on the Nevsky Prospect, but now it has been destroyed
because the owners are German. How awful it all is!

One good thing: I don't have to study my German lessons
anymore! Of course that still leaves Russian, English, and

French. What a bore. Why couldn't I have been born already <u>knowing</u> all these languages!

Christmas Eve 1914

Papa is home. It's so good to have us all gathered here together again, the way it used to be. As usual, Papa wanted *kutia*, a kind of cereal made of rice and raisins, served in a bowl set in the middle of a mound of hay that symbolizes the Holy Nativity in the manger. Then we had our Christmas Eve dinner: almond soup and poached carp.

Before, we always stepped outside to offer greetings to Papa's subjects who had gathered in front of Alexander Palace to wish us a joyous Christmas. But we're not making any public appearances like those of last summer, because many people are upset and angry. They thought the war would be over by now, and they're blaming Papa.

They also blame everything German. Mama's friend Lili Dehn says the orchestras in Petrograd are forbidden to play music by any German composers. So when we got together to put on our little musical program, I wasn't allowed to play that pretty song I've practiced so hard: It's called "Für Elise," by Beethoven. And Tatiana may not play the "Moonlight Sonata" by the same composer.

But I can't seem to help <u>whistling</u> "Für Elise" and don't even realize I'm doing it. Mama says it's naughty, and that I must stop.

Christmas 1914

Mama is smiling again because Father Grigory has come to visit us before he returns to his village in Siberia. Papa treats him very politely, even though it's well known that Father Grigory tried to convince Papa to stay out of the war.

Lots of gifts for everybody. Mama gave us each an icon of the Blessed Virgin, and Papa gave us bracelets set with pearls. I tinted photographs that I've taken of the family for Papa to carry with him when he goes back to *Stavka*.

After dinner, Alexei entertained us with his balalaika. All Russian music and very cheering.

28 December 1914/10 January 1915

Something odd is going on here. I think Mashka is falling in love with one of the palace guards. I catch her gazing out the window at one in particular. I must find out his name.

2/15 January 1915

Awful news: Anya Vyrubova was in a terrible train wreck. Mama and Papa got word that she was hurt so badly, she may die. They rushed to Petrograd to be with her in her last hours. We are all praying for her.

4/17 January 1915

Anya is not only alive, she is getting better! This is what happened:

As soon as Mama heard about Anya, she sent Father Grigory a telegram, and he rushed to the hospital. Anya was in a delirium when he arrived, and the doctors said there was nothing to be done. Her legs had been crushed and her head pinned under a steel girder.

But Father Grigory brushed the doctors away and took her hand. "Annushka!" he called out three times. Anya slowly opened her eyes. Then he ordered her to rise, and she tried to obey him. Next he ordered her to speak to him, and she did!

Everyone in the room was astonished. She will live, Father Grigory told them, but she will always be crippled. Then he left the room and collapsed.

Mama and Papa both believe it's a miracle. I do, too.

10/23 January 1915

The guard that Mashka's been admiring is Nicholas Dmitrievitch Demekov, and he's from Moscow. I asked Dunyasha's daughter Natasha, and she told me his name. Natasha planned to get married this month, but her Vladya volunteered for the front, and the wedding is postponed.

24 January/6 February 1915

Anya is out of the hospital. Her house is only a summer place and is freezing cold, so she's staying in the palace with us. Papa has not gone back to *Stavka*, and will be at home until the fighting resumes in the spring. Mama and the Big Pair still have much to do at the hospitals, and they have hardly any time or energy left to look after Anya, so Mashka and I will visit her every day.

25 January/7 February 1915

Today is the first day of Butterweek, and we took Anya lots of blini drenched in butter. Alexei went with us, and it's hard to say who ate more blini, Anya or Alexei. But she grows fatter, and he doesn't.

Anya says if the war goes on much longer, there will be no more butter and a shortage of many other things, but the imperial family (us) will not have to do without. Knowing Mama, though, I'm pretty sure she'll want us to share the fate of the Russian people. If they have to do without butter, then so will we.

3/16 February 1915

The Great Fast began yesterday. As usual, I spent time with Anya Vyrubova. She's very easy to entertain, as long as we talk about Father Grigory. She's convinced he's a saint. Mama believes it, too, because Alexei always gets better when Father Grigory prays over him. Anya also believes Father Grigory has a divine purpose: that God sent him to save our family and all of Holy Russia. She says that only God knows how.

He does not smell as bad as he used to (<u>stink</u> is a better word), but he still makes me feel very strange. I want so much to talk to Mashka about him, and to ask her what she thinks, but I don't dare.

———•◆•———

5/18 February 1915

Well, I <u>did</u> dare to ask Mashka what she thinks about Father Grigory. She looked at me with her big blue eyes and said, "But he <u>is</u> a saint!" Then she said that if he smells nasty and has dirty fingernails and looks at us in that way he does, as though he can see straight into our souls, it's because God is testing our faith.

Dear Mashka, she is so good! I must be evil to my very bones, because <u>I do not like this man</u>, no matter what anyone says.

13/26 February 1915

Papa left today for *Stavka*, and we are all feeling very sad — especially Alexei. But Papa was in a jolly mood, full of optimism for the spring offensive. Two million new recruits are headed for the front lines — enough, surely, to bring victory soon.

18 February/3 March 1915

Our tutors insist that we study geography. Every morning we stare at maps of Russia, especially west of the Ural Mountains, as well as of Hungary and Austria and Poland, where the fighting is going on. We have bunches of little pins, white for the Russian army, black for the Germans, yellow for the Austrians, and so on, and when we have news of their location in the war, we move the pins around on the map.

And while we wait for news, we still have our exercises in math, English, French, etc. As if it matters.

21 February/6 March 1915

Alexei came up with a brilliant idea — using Papa's bathing pool while Papa is away. Not to be outdone, I insisted that we girls also be allowed to use the bathing pool as well. So Mama wrote to Papa and got his permission, and in we went. And it was such fun! We had a terrific time, jumping into the water and swimming around. Why haven't we thought of it before?

23 February/8 March 1915

We're attacking the Austrian province of Galicia. I know exactly where it is — it used to be part of Poland — and moved our pins.

25 February/10 March 1915

Poor Mama! I feel so sad for her. Since November she has had a close attachment to a young soldier in her care at the hospital. Often he was entirely off his head and sometimes thought she was his mother or an angel or both. He died this morning, and we all wept for him. His name was Ivan, and he was exactly Olga's age.

3/16 March 1915

Father Grigory is here, speaking privately with Mama. She says she needs his advice on keeping things running smoothly with Papa away at *Stavka*.

----·•·----

6/19 March 1915

Ha! Victory! Lots of prisoners and guns taken at a fortress in Galicia. Alexei knows the numbers of each, but I don't. I'm happy just to move our white pins forward.

Mama says Papa is very pleased with Grand Duke Nicholas Nicholaievitch, the commander-in-chief, and gave him a gold sword with a diamond-covered hilt to celebrate the grand victory. Mama speaks about it with her lips pressed into a thin line, so I can tell she doesn't believe the grand duke deserves such a reward. For some reason, she doesn't like him much.

8/21 March 1915

Anya Vyrubova is such a gossip! Thank goodness, because otherwise I would never know what's happening. Mashka and I were playing duets for her (no German music, thank you!), and when we stopped for tea, Anya told us that she loathes Grand Duke Nicholas Nicholaievitch. Here's her reason: "Because the grand duke despises our Grishka!" (Grishka is what she calls Father Grigory.)

Then, because Anya was in an especially talkative mood, I asked her if she knew why the grand duke despises Father

Grigory. According to her, it's because he doesn't believe that Father Grigory is a true man of God. The grand duke, and many other ignorant people, she says, claim that Father Grigory is a charlatan who only pretends to be deeply religious but in fact lives a wicked life of debauchery and dissolution and dissipation. (She also used other words that I didn't understand and can't spell.) Anya says that these same ignorant people believe that Father Grigory has too much influence over Mama, and that he is seeking power for himself. Then she said, "I think the people who malign our Grishka are jealous of him."

I said nothing, but I wonder: What if they're right?

15/28 March 1915
Palm Sunday

Papa has come home for Easter, and he's in a splendid mood because he says we're winning the war. But when I ask him <u>when</u>, he shakes his head and says, "In God's time." That means he doesn't know.

22 March/4 April 1915

Easter

A year ago we were in Livadia. I looked back in my diary and read about the happy times we were having. Now everything is changed. One of Mama's friends sent us a whole carload of spring flowers from the Crimea — peonies, irises, violets, wisteria. That cheered us but also reminded us of what we're missing.

The Easter egg that Papa gave Mama this year is white enamel with a red cross, opening to show paintings of Mama, Olga, Tatiana, Aunt Olga, and cousin Marie in their nurse uniforms. This is the plainest Fabergé egg I've ever seen, but Mama says it is appropriate for wartime.

Papa leaves again in a few days for *Stavka*. The Russians are on the attack in the Carpathian Mountains in Poland. Alexei will have more prisoners to count, and I will have more pins to move.

30 March/12 April 1915

Although we are winning battles and the Austrian army is on the run, there are many wounded soldiers still arriving daily at the hospitals. As Mama says, every foot of ground we gain is paid for in Russian blood.

In his last letter, Papa said he hoped we were being diligent in keeping our diaries, because it's good discipline. It would displease Papa immensely to know that I don't write as regularly as I used to. But it's just too hard to write when we're all feeling so sad.

5/18 April 1915

We had a concert this afternoon in our hospital. An old man told amusing stories, and a lady performed a Russian folk dance. I thought the dancer seemed much too pleased with herself, but the soldiers were happy, so I suppose it was a great success.

But here was the best thing: Nicholas Dmitrievitch Demekov was there and introduced the performers to us. Now I know for sure: Mashka is mad about him! It's "Kolya says this" and "Kolya thinks that" all the time, and she thinks I don't notice how she looks at him. It's rather disgusting. He's not even that handsome, although I suppose you could say he's rather sweet.

———•—•———

20 April/3 May 1915

Oh, those vile Germans! Yesterday — and on a Sunday, at that — the German artillery opened fire on our men at the front in Poland. Thousands of Russians were killed and wounded, and the trains are bringing the survivors to Mama's hospitals. Among those to arrive was Natasha's Vladya. Mama says his condition is grave.

6/19 May 1915

Papa's birthday. We are so sad without him.

21 May/3 June 1915

The Germans are winning more and more battles. All through Poland the black pins are overwhelming the white pins on our map.

This is the first summer we haven't gone on a cruise on the *Standart*, but everyone is too busy here. I do miss the sea. I try not to think about it, because it's useless.

23 May/5 June 1915

I saw a newspaper on Professor Petrov's desk and managed to read some of the headlines before the paper vanished. In Moscow a great mob was calling for the tsar to give up his throne and turn it over to Grand Duke Nicholas Nicholaievitch. I do understand now why Mama dislikes the commander-in-chief, but what I don't understand is what people could have against Papa.

29 May/11 June 1915

Mama has a letter from Aunt Ella in Moscow. She says that mobs broke into a piano store and began throwing grand pianos out of the windows because they had been made by German companies.

Then an angry crowd went to the Convent of Martha and Mary, which Aunt Ella founded many years ago after her husband was killed. They accused Aunt Ella of hiding our uncle Erni there, which is ridiculous, because of course he's in Germany. She did as Mama would have done and bravely faced them down, even though someone threw a big stone at her.

It's Tatiana's birthday. She's eighteen. I gathered some flowers for her and put them by her plate at breakfast, and Anya has invited us for tea tomorrow.

5/18 June 1915

Today is my fourteenth birthday. On the day before my birthday last year, I wrote, "Tomorrow is the day that everything will change. If I keep saying that, I'm sure it will." What I meant was, everything would get <u>better</u>.

I know it's wicked of me to complain, because Mama, Papa, and Tatiana have all had birthdays in the past few weeks, and they <u>never</u> complain.

I got a beautiful diamond for my necklace. In two years it will be complete, and I'll have a lovely party like Olga's. Tatiana and Mashka will have theirs when the war is over. Mama has promised.

But here's what I wanted: a ride in the country in Monsieur Gilliard's automobile. But Monsieur Gilliard says it's too dangerous and promises that next year I'll get my wish. That's what everybody says, "Next year, Anastasia Nicholaievna."

To which I say: Faugh! (I don't say *Pfui* anymore, because it's German.)

14/27 June 1915

Mashka's birthday, her sixteenth. She got the last diamond needed for her necklace.

26 June/9 July 1915

Papa has been home for a week, and he's very restless. He says that only when he's with the soldiers does he feel he's helping to beat the filthy Germans. Mama, on the other hand, is glad to get him away from the grand duke. The rest of us are merely ecstatic to have him with us.

4/17 July 1915

We had tea today at Anya's house. She uses crutches or a wheelchair to get about, but at least she's alive. She invited some of the officers to join us, including Mashka's Kolya. They gaze at each other like sick puppies. I can hardly stand to watch them.

23 July/5 August 1915

Terrible news. We were having tea on the balcony, where Mama likes to sit in the open air, and Papa came out of his study. He was trembling so badly he could hardly stand. We all stared at him.

"Warsaw has fallen," he said, and sat down sobbing. "It cannot go on like this," he repeated over and over, his head buried in his hands.

I've never seen Papa in such a state. Naturally, I burst into tears, too. I didn't have to look at a map to see why this loss is so important. Warsaw is the capital of the part of Poland that belongs to Russia.

30 July/12 August 1915

Today is Alexei's eleventh birthday. We tried to make it a happy day for him, with all his favorite foods (he can't get enough blini) and a pile of new toys — mostly wooden guns and toy soldiers. When he is well, he marches around the park with a gun over his shoulder, and when he's ill he lines up the lead soldiers on his bedcovers and fights mock battles.

Even while we were celebrating, we could tell that Papa and Mama are worried and distracted. But what can anyone do?

8/21 August 1915

Two days ago Papa and Mama made a private trip to Petrograd with only a few aides. When they came back, they told us they had been praying for guidance before the tombs of the tsars.

As a result, Papa has decided to take over as commander-in-chief, in place of Grand Duke Nicholas Nicholaievitch. Mama is pleased, even though it means Papa will spend all his time at *Stavka*. He says we may come there to visit him often, but this doesn't comfort Alexei, who lies in bed with his face to the wall.

16/29 August 1915

Papa has gone. At nine o'clock every morning, Mama goes into Papa's study and receives some of the same ministers and government representatives who used to come to talk to Papa! It's almost as though she's the tsar.

Meanwhile, my brother and sisters and I must have our same old dreary lessons. Unfair, in my opinion.

10/23 September 1915

Mama hardly has time to help us decide what clothes to wear. Olga and Tatiana dress in their gray Red Cross uniforms. Before they leave for the hospital, Tatiana picks out the dresses, shoes, hats, and so on that Mashka and I must put on. She's so bossy that we call her "the Governess." She even tells Olga what to do, and Olga does it!

Father Grigory is here almost every day now. He and Mama talk over all kinds of things, because with Papa away it is up to Mama to look after the government. She says Father Grigory's advice is better than anybody else's, and she trusts him completely because he's a man of God. "Just look what he's done for Baby and for Anya." And that's true.

(But I don't think Alexei likes it when Mama calls him Baby. He would much rather be called Your Imperial Highness, or some other grand title.)

---

26 September/9 October 1915

Papa came home and announced another big decision: He's taking Alexei to *Stavka* with him. It's breaking Mama's heart to send "Baby" away, but she believes it will be good for Papa and good for Alexei in the long run.

1/14 October 1915

Such an emotional day. We went to the railroad station to see off Papa and Alexei. We were all in tears, but I was not weeping too hard, because M. Gilliard and Mr. Gibbes went with them, and I won't be plagued with French and English lessons while they're gone. That leaves Professor Petrov, but I can always get my way with him.

25 October/7 November 1915

Mashka's Kolya was at Mass today. Somehow she managed to sit so they could look sideways at each other and exchange smiles. It is <u>so</u> amusing, but she gets furious when I tease her.

14/27 November 1915

Papa and Alexei spent weeks touring the front lines. From all reports, Alexei adored every minute of it, but Mama was beside herself with worry the whole time. Now we hear that they're safely back at *Stavka*, and Mama is more at ease.

19 November/2 December 1915

This is so disgusting! There's a mouse in our bedroom. I can hear it scratching around at night, and twice I've seen it dart under the bed. I'm thinking of borrowing Alexei's pussycat and putting her to work.

4/17 December 1915

Alexei's problems have worsened, and he's been brought home again from *Stavka*. How disappointed he is! It began with a cold, and when Alexei had a sneezing fit, he developed a nosebleed. The doctor couldn't stop it, and it went from bad to worse. M. Gilliard rode with him on the train, and I heard him tell Professor Petrov that there were several times on the journey when he had feared my brother was truly dying.

Now Alexei is feeling better, and all he can talk about is his life with the army, and how he was allowed to sit in on important meetings with Papa and review the troops with Papa and so on. All this is to get him ready for the day when he will become tsar.

I play cards with him by the hour, to try to cheer him up. When he isn't hurting, he demands to know when he can go back to *Stavka*.

6/19 December 1915

Father Grigory came today, at Mama's request. As always, Alexei seems much better after his visit. It's so cold here that we can't keep warm. Inspired by the freezing weather inside the palace, Alexei is knitting a scarf, using whatever bits and pieces of colored wool we can find for him. I taught him the stitches, and it keeps him quiet and contented.

Today is Papa's name day, in honor of St. Nicholas, and Father Vasilev gave him a special blessing at lunch.

7/20 December 1915

Baroness Buxhoeveden organized a cinema in the main hall of the hospital yesterday, and Mashka and I helped wheel the wounded in so that they could watch the films. Only one of the films was truly funny. I wonder why they don't show more funny ones.

9/22 December 1915

Alexei's knitted scarf grows longer and longer. We are kept busy hunting for wool for it.

12/25 December 1915

Late this afternoon Papa kissed us all and left again for *Stavka*. He says we must get used to his absence, that it's a small sacrifice to make for Russia, and reminds us of the poor boys in our hospitals who are far from home.

19 December 1915/1 January 1916

Poor Mama is in bed, miserable with a toothache. Her cheek is badly swollen.

25 December 1915/7 January 1916
Christmas

This seems almost like any other day, except we exchanged gifts. I was afraid that Alexei would give his famous scarf to one of us and then we would have to wear it so as not to hurt his feelings. But he says it's for his new puppy, Joy. Thank goodness, because it's quite ugly, and I feel partly responsible.

29 December 1915/11 January 1916

Joy shares my opinion of the scarf. It's two meters long — or was, until the puppy decided to unknit it. Now it's a pile of unraveled yarn, and Alexei is in tears. Good sister that I am, I promised to help him mend it.

2/15 January 1916

Alexei is better, but still needs lots of rest. He keeps asking when he can go back to *Stavka* with Papa, but no one will answer that.

He asked me to write in his diary while he dictates what to put down. Papa told him that keeping a diary is important for a future tsar, but Alexei is lazy and wants someone else to do it for him.

22 January/4 February 1916

Some sailors from the *Standart* have begun to build a snow mountain in our park. "The higher the better!" I tell them, and they laugh and promise to make it as high as the Ural Mountains.

27 January/9 February 1916

We were supposed to help with the snow mountain, but instead we threw snowballs at the sailors, keeping them from their work. I took photographs of all of them.

31 January/13 February 1916

Anya was inspired to arrange a concert at her hospital this afternoon. The star was a sweet little ten-year-old girl who performed a Russian folk dance, accompanied by a concertina. Very popular.

3/16 February 1916

The sailors spent the day carrying water from under the ice of the pond and hauling it to the top of the snow mountain. It froze almost as quickly as it was poured, and we'll now have a fine place to run our sleds.

I think I'm coming down with a cold.

8/21 February 1916

Mashka is in such a state! She has just learned that her Kolya is leaving in a few weeks, and she has decided to sew him a shirt as a farewell present. I said I thought Alexei would probably be happy to knit him a scarf like Joy's, and she told me not to make jokes. Kolya is going to the front, and no one knows when she'll see him again. I think she really does care for him, and I'm sorry I teased her.

15/28 February 1916

Butterweek! The chef managed to get all the butter we wanted for our blini. I must have eaten two dozen. Tatiana looks at me sharply. "A good thing you'll now have seven weeks of fasting," she says. Nasty thing! Just because she is slim as a willow!

24 February/8 March 1916

My sisters and I had a glorious time racing our sleds down our snow mountain, but poor Alexei was not even allowed to come watch. Mama's orders. She's desperately afraid he'll hurt himself, since even a minor injury turns into a major one for Alexei. If Papa were here, he would take Alexei's side and insist that he be allowed, with Derevenko or Nagorny to keep close watch on him. But Papa <u>isn't</u> here, and Mama rules.

Father Grigory came for dinner. I asked to be excused as soon as I could get away with it.

26 February/10 March 1916

We went for a drive in the *troika* after tea today, but without the little bells on the three horses (forbidden during the Great Fast), a sleigh ride is not so much fun.

Kolya leaves tomorrow. Mashka had the shirt she made delivered to him, and he called her on the telephone to thank her and to say good-bye. I don't know what else they talked about, because when I tried to listen, Mashka looked cross and shooed me away.

13/26 March 1916

Anya's weekly concert featured a pair of acrobats, a father and his son who performed incredible feats. We held our breath and could hardly keep from crying out. I had the awful feeling that Alexei would want to try some of their exploits. Apparently Mama was thinking the same thing, for she lectured him quite sternly about it and warned Derevenko to keep a sharp watch over him.

19 March/1 April 1916

Natasha's Vladya died during the night. She's inconsolable, poor thing.

2/15 April 1916

Papa will not be spending Easter with us! The Feast of Feasts, the greatest day of the whole year, and he's off with his troops. As I complained bitterly about this, Alexei looked at me scathingly and said, "This is war. The tsar's place is with his troops."

Alexei is aching to be back at *Stavka* with Papa, and Mama says she'll allow him to go in a few weeks if he doesn't injure himself.

This is one way to keep him off the snow mountain.

10/23 April 1916
Easter

The procession on Good Friday was very beautiful and very moving. Round and round the church we walked, behind the chanting priests, the air so still that we didn't have to shield the candle flames with our hands. Last night, after the midnight service, we ate kulich with sweet cheese but without Papa here, it didn't taste nearly so good. People sent us Easter eggs of various kinds, and Mama and Papa had porcelain eggs made to give to army officers. Mama's Fabergé egg is made of steel, mounted on four bullet shapes. Papa says it's called the Military Egg. In my opinion it's very ugly.

It's been two years since we spent Easter at Livadia, but I have made up my mind not to mention it. My sisters say I whine a lot. I must show them how brave and uncomplaining I am!

20 April/3 May 1916

Papa is home for a short stay. He'll take Alexei back to *Stavka* with him.

4/17 May 1916

How quiet it seems! Papa is gone; Alexei, too, Monsieur Gilliard, and Mr. Gibbes with them. There is such a thing as <u>too much</u> quiet.

The trees are starting to turn green again. Mama says this is a sign of God's love for us.

Tatiana and Olga lounge on their windowsill and sunbathe. Also — the snow mountain is slowly melting.

7/20 May 1916

Suddenly the sun disappeared, it's raining, and once again we're shivering and reaching for our shawls. I'm sure we're all thinking of Livadia, but none of us mentions it. Since it's so unpleasant outside, Mashka and I are practicing playing musical instruments together. She plays the piano, and I play the balalaika. We sound quite good, and I've suggested that we perform at one of Anya's Sunday afternoon concerts. I'm sure the soldiers would find us delightful.

14/27 May 1916

We've received the dearest letter from Alexei — he's been promoted to the rank of corporal, and he's as proud as though he were a general! Mama says we may all go to *Stavka* for Alexei's birthday. But that's almost three months away!

21 May/3 June 1916

Glorious weather. There's just one small heap of dirty snow left from our snow mountain where the sun does not strike it.

The park and palace grounds have become overgrown and neglected because so many of the groundskeepers are away at war. We've been pulling weeds that are choking out the lilies of the valley. The lilacs are in bloom, and we've gathered armloads of them and arranged them in Mama's boudoir. I feel very virtuous when I do such work, as though I were a peasant. That's rather fun, at times.

28 May/10 June 1916

The news from the front is tremendously encouraging. The new offensive begun last week in Galicia (that's southern Poland) was a complete triumph. Now, on to Vienna! Mama says the tide of the war is definitely turning in our favor. I hope so, because I'm completely sick of it.

5/18 June 1916

I am fifteen years old.

My life has changed, but not in ways that I had hoped it would. For one thing, Mama seems not to have noticed that I'm growing up. She still seems to think we're all children. Mashka will be seventeen in a few days (Kolya sent her a card, which she refused to show me); Tatiana just turned nineteen; and Olga will be twenty-one in November!

My favorite birthday gift (aside from another diamond for the necklace I'm to get next year) is a table-tennis set. I make my sisters play with me, but Mashka complains that she must spend too much time down on the floor looking for balls that go off the table.

20 June/3 July 1916

Such fun Mashka and I had today! We strung a hammock between two trees near the path by the balcony. We got in it together and started rocking, back and forth, until it turned over. I fell out flat on my face, but Mashka hung on like a monkey and laughed herself silly. Next, it was my turn, and I paid her back!

2/15 July 1916

Monsieur Gilliard is on leave and came to dinner with us. It was nice to have him here as a friend and not as a tutor. After dinner, he chatted with us while I knitted and my sisters sewed madly on shirts for officers who are leaving the hospital soon to return to the fighting at the front. I pray with all my soul that they will be safe and not be brought back to us again.

30 July/12 August 1916
Stavka

As promised, we're here to celebrate Alexei's twelfth birthday. We went sailing on the Dnieper River on a sweet little yacht, and we all made a great fuss over Alexei with lots of presents, but he seems more grown up and serious.

Such fun, living on our train again, although it is rather hot. The train station is far from town, and we have nowhere to go except out into the countryside, where we visit with the peasants and feed sweets to the adorable children who follow us around like puppies. We feel so much freer here than we do in Tsarskoe Selo.

If Mama and the Big Pair didn't have so much work at their hospital, we could come more often. When I grumbled about that, Mama told me I must not be selfish but think of those who are sacrificing so much. That made me feel guilty — exactly what Mama intended, I suppose.

———◆———

12/25 September 1916

Ts. S.

No matter how many promises I make to myself, I keep forgetting to write in this diary. Maybe <u>forgetting</u> is not the right word. It seems that everything I have to put down is either discouraging (Romania has declared war on Germany, and Papa is very worried) or boring (lessons) or just silly. Maybe today I'll write about something silly, such as the new game we've made up: riding our bicycles at breakneck speed through the palace halls. By "we," I mean Mashka and me. Tatiana is too sensible to indulge in such foolishness, and Olga is always too busy reading some book or other. So far we've had several spectacular crashes but amazingly have not yet broken a single thing.

17/30 October 1916

War news hasn't been good lately, and I don't want to write about it because today is supposed to be a celebration — the second anniversary of the founding of the hospital here at the Great Palace. There was a concert this afternoon by the orchestra from the *Standart*. I recognized lots of the pieces they used to play on the yacht, and it made all of us feel sad — including, I think, the musicians.

21 October/3 November 1916

Olga has gotten a kitten, an adorable little thing. She wears a blue ribbon with a tiny bell around her neck. Maybe this will put an end to our mouse roommates, who came back as soon as the weather turned cold. Alexei's cat proved much too lazy for the job, and when Alexei went to stay at *Stavka*, it ran away and has never been seen again. Actually it was a bad-tempered thing, and I don't miss it.

More awful news about the war. The Germans have occupied most of Romania, and Papa has ordered troops to try to save Bucharest, the capital. To think that Olga might be there now if she had married Prince Carol!

27 October/9 November 1916

Papa is taking Alexei to visit Grandmother in Kiev, where she now lives. I used to complain sometimes about her formal Sunday luncheons, where I was expected to behave perfectly and speak French and eat all kinds of foreign food, but now I miss her very much and would even eat those snails if she asked me to.

2/15 November 1916

Papa and Alexei came here from Kiev, and both are in a black mood. Alexei complains that Papa was gruff with him (and Papa is never gruff!). I have even heard Mama and Papa exchange sharp words. The subject is Father Grigory. Mama gets lots of help and advice from him when Papa is away, and Papa doesn't agree with that advice. He says that Father Grigory may be a saint and a miracle worker, but he is not the tsar and should not tell Mama which government leaders to dismiss and whom to appoint. I'm not supposed to know any of this.

23 November/6 December 1916

Papa is home, and as a special treat he and Mama are attending the ballet in Petrograd. My sisters and I are going, and Anya, too! We're very excited, for since the war began we haven't attended any balls or parties or done anything at all exciting.

Alexei isn't going. He can't walk well just now, and it would cause too much gossip if the tsarevitch had to be carried by one of the sailors. I'm a little afraid that at the last moment Mama and Papa will decide that <u>none</u> of us should go, because that would cause less attention than if only the tsarevitch is missing.

24 November/7 December 1916

The ballet was absolutely enchanting! The Maryinski Theater is so pretty, with gold brocade and red velvet everywhere. Mama wore a beautiful gown of ice-blue satin embroidered with pearls, we wore blue velvet, and Anya wore a gown that might have looked better as a lamp shade. (I mentioned this to Tatiana, who says I am too cruel for words. But she was laughing.)

We watched the Imperial Ballet perform *Pharoah's Daughter*. The *prima ballerina assoluta*, Mathilde Kschessinska, is the most beautiful dancer in the world. A young ballet student played the part of a monkey and leaped around in the tops of make-believe trees until Kschessinska shot him down with a make-believe arrow. After the performance the boy came to our box to be presented to Papa and Mama, who gave him a silver box of chocolates. The boy could hardly speak, he was so overcome — he just stared.

After the ballet we had a late supper with Anya.

5/18 December 1916

Papa called from *Stavka* with the dreadful news that Bucharest has fallen to the enemy. I can't bear to move the pins on the map one more time.

8/21 December 1916

Aunt Ella has come from Moscow to visit Mama and plans to stay for several days. We're so happy to have her here, because it does get lonely at times since we hardly ever go anywhere and Papa is rarely here.

9/22 December 1916

We've just seen Aunt Ella off at the railroad station. She stayed less than one day.

Here's what happened: The real reason Aunt Ella came was not just for a family visit but to speak seriously to Mama about Father Grigory. Our aunt believes that Father

Grigory is not a real holy man at all but a fraud, and that he's giving Mama bad advice. I heard her with my own ears: "Rasputin, that man you call <u>holy</u>, has pushed Russia to the brink of disaster." She told Mama that the country is in chaos, the peasants are starving, and the army is threatening rebellion. She even said there are revolutionaries who want to depose Papa and take over the country.

And then she started ticking off all the bad advice that Father Grigory has given to Mama. Mostly it has to do with getting rid of certain officials that Father Grigory doesn't like, or who don't like him, and naming others to replace them. And the ones Mama appointed, Aunt Ella says, are incompetent and weak and make matters worse.

But Mama refused to listen. She says she knows that lots of people disapprove of Father Grigory, and that many actually hate him. But Mama knows who he truly is, a saint, and she will not listen to lies about him, and not for anything in the world will she send him away.

Since Mama would not listen to her, even for a minute, Aunt Ella went back to Moscow. She and Mama were both crying.

—◆—

18/31 December 1916

Father Grigory is missing. No one can find him, and Mama expects the worst. She's convinced he was murdered by an assassin. She says he often told her, "If I die or you desert me, you will lose your son and your crown within six months." And she believes that.

It's so terrible, I can't write about it.

19 December 1916/1 January 1917

Father Grigory is dead. His body was found under the ice of the Neva River in Petrograd. Papa has come home from *Stavka*, and Mama is nearly hysterical with grief. I know her greatest fear: Now there is no one who can help Alexei with his illness. The assassin is Prince Felix Yussupov, who is married to Papa's niece, Princess Irina, the sister of all those horrid boy cousins. The prince is so handsome, I can hardly believe that he could have done such a horrible thing, even though he claims he killed Rasputin for the good of Russia. He was helped by one of Papa's favorite cousins, Dmitri Pavlovitch. And there were others, too. Papa intends to banish them from Petrograd forever.

I feel sorry for every bad thing I ever said or even thought about Father Grigory.

21 December 1916/3 January 1917

Today was one of the saddest days I remember, the day of Father Grigory's funeral. His body was brought here secretly from Petrograd and prepared for burial. We drove to our church in a closed car, all of us dressed entirely in black. Before we left the palace, we signed our names on the back of a small icon of the Virgin Mary that Mama then placed on the breast of the corpse before the coffin was sealed. She gave us white flowers to scatter on top of the coffin. Then Father Grigory's body was buried in the park, near the spot where Anya is building a chapel. Poor Mama. Poor Papa. Poor everybody.

24 December 1916/6 January 1917

It's Christmas Eve. We've exchanged some little hand-made gifts and given presents to the staff, but we're all too upset to celebrate in any way. We sit and stare out at the falling snow.

28 December 1916/10 January 1917

Papa doesn't want to see anyone or speak with anyone. He's very nervous and distraught and smokes one cigarette after another. Mama and Anya hold each other's hands and weep. Alexei's arm hurts him. The doctors do what they can, but there is no Father Grigory to call when it gets really bad.

19 January/1 February 1917

I just don't feel like writing. Everyone and everything is bleak and gloomy.

4/17 February 1917

Olga and Tatiana are both ill with measles. I've been sitting in their darkened room to keep them company. Mama's friend Lili Dehn came to try to cheer us up. She doesn't have an easy task.

To distract us all, Papa reads to us, mostly stories by Chekhov.

9/22 February 1917

Not feeling well. Headache. I hope it's not measles.

17 February/2 March 1917

I do have measles. So does Alexei. And Anya, too! Anya complains more than all of us put together. Tatiana has pain in her ears, and her head is bandaged, so she can't hear a thing. Olga's cough is so bad, she can't speak. Mashka is still all right. Mama has all she can do to take care of us. Lili Dehn is staying with us, sleeping on the sofa in the Red Room, to be near us all. Papa went back to *Stavka* to see what can be done. He told us to be brave, and we promised, but we all burst into tears the minute he was gone.

25 February/10 March 1917

Revolutionaries have taken over the whole city of Petrograd. It's hard for me to understand this. Lili tries to explain that people are suffering from the war and want it to end. (We all do!) She says there are men who insist that Papa doesn't know how to win the war and doesn't care for the Russian people. Even the soldiers in Petrograd are turning against the tsar. This is what Aunt Ella was trying to warn Mama about.

Papa called to say he's coming home. He reminded us again to be brave, but I'm too frightened to sleep.

1/14 March 1917

Where is Papa? We're frantic. He should be here by now. We know only that he couldn't get through Petrograd to reach us because the revolutionaries control the railroad station. The water and electricity have been cut off, and the telephone lines as well.

Baroness Buxhoeveden arrived in a hysterical state, saying that a sentry has been killed not five hundred meters from the palace. Mama and Mashka (the only one of us who is not dreadfully sick) put on heavy coats and went out to plead with the palace guards to remain calm. I was terrified that something would happen to them, but they returned safely, and I thank God for that. The rebellious soldiers have agreed to establish a neutral zone. Everything seems calm again. But I'm not.

3/16 March 1917

Still no word from Papa. A blizzard swirls around us, the wind howling and the snow so thick, we can't see anything outside our windows.

We've heard sickening rumors that Papa has abdicated. That mean he's no longer tsar. But who will be tsar now? Alexei is still too young. Mama would never allow it.

4/17 March 1917

I will never forget this day as long as I live. Papa managed to get through to Mama by telephone and confirm the rumors: He has abdicated. Two days ago he informed the Duma, the elected assembly, that he would abdicate in favor of his son. But then he realized that Alexei is too frail, and that he would be taken away from us. So Papa changed his mind and abdicated in favor of Uncle Misha, his brother Mikhail Alexandrovitch. But then Uncle Misha abdicated as well, and now there is no tsar.

Mama, weeping, turned to us and said, "The first part has come true, just as Father Grigory predicted. We have lost the crown."

5/18 March 1917

Papa is on his way home. He told us that the Duma has set up something called a provisional government. I don't know what this means. On the advice of Lili, Mama is burning her diaries, started before any of us were born. A great fire is roaring in the grate in the Red Room, and one by one she feeds the books into the flames.

I don't know what my sisters will do, but I have resolved never to burn mine.

8/21 March 1917

We are under arrest! General Kornilov of the Provisional Government arrived, demanding to speak to Mama. (I saw him; he's unbelievably ugly.) He told her that he's doing this to protect us from the revolutionary soldiers, and that after Papa comes we'll all go to Murmansk, and a British cruiser will take us to England. When the general left, Mama came to tell us this horrible news. Tatiana is still quite deaf, so I had to write down for her what Mama said.

After he talked to Mama, the general spoke to the palace guards and the palace staff and told them they could leave if they wanted, but if they stay, they will be under house arrest with us. Most have already gone.

The regular guards have all deserted, and the soldiers who came in their place have been firing their rifles in the park. I think they're shooting the deer.

The palace doors are locked. We are prisoners.

9/22 March 1917

Papa is back, at last. We were so glad to see him that we wept. So did Mama, and so did he. All we do is cry.

11/24 March 1917

Our hair has begun to fall out, whether from the disease or from the medicines, I don't know. Mama decided the best thing is to shave our heads, and now we're all as bald as baby birds. It's so funny! It's the only thing we have to laugh at.

We're all feeling better except Mashka, who now has measles and pneumonia on top of it. Thank goodness Dr. Botkin and Dr. Derevenko are staying with us after so many others decided to leave.

Others who are still here: Anya, of course, and dear Lili; two of Mama's ladies-in-waiting, Baroness Buxhoeveden and Countess Hendrikov; Count Benckendorff and his wife; and Prince Dolgoruky; also M. Gilliard and Mr. Gibbes. Professor Petrov is gone without a farewell.

Sailor Derevenko left, but not before he treated Alexei very badly. He's been with my brother since Alexei was just beginning to walk, and we always thought Derevenko was devoted. But as soon as Papa abdicated, Sailor Derevenko began ordering Alexei to run little errands, as though <u>he</u> were the tsarevitch and Alexei his servant! Now I wonder how many other people that I thought truly cared for us have been waiting for a chance to be as mean and heartless as possible. At least Sailor Nagorny still seems loyal.

I wanted to <u>kick</u> Derevenko, but he was gone before I got a chance.

18/31 March 1917

If I'm going to keep on writing in this diary, I must not start every entry with "a horrible thing happened" or "this is terrible" or "that person behaved rudely." But it's true! The soldiers who came to guard us have no manners at all. I found two in our bathroom this morning, taking the cap off the tooth powder and shaking it out as though they had never used a toothbrush. And when our doctors come to treat us, those loutish soldiers barge right into our bedrooms to watch.

21 March/3 April 1917

I promised I would not say "this terrible thing," but this is <u>truly</u> terrible: Anya and Lili were arrested today. It was raining, and we watched from the window of Alexei's room as they were driven away. We have no idea what will happen to them and are sick with worry.

The man who took them was the minister of justice, Alexander Feodorovitch Kerensky. He has a face like a rat. Papa says we may expect to see more of him, that our fate is in his hands.

Papa is also worried about Grandmother. She visited him at Petrograd for a short time after he announced that he was abdicating. She told him she was leaving for the Crimea, and of course we're all praying that she got there safely.

22 March/4 April 1917

We've learned a bit more: Lili and Anya were taken to Petrograd, where Lili was released and Anya imprisoned at the Fortress of Peter and Paul. We have no idea why

Anya was kept and Lili let go. It's frightening not to know the reasons.

24 March/6 April 1917

We've had a letter from Grandmother. Her train got through safely to the Crimea, and she's at her palace on the Black Sea. My aunt Olga has recently married, and she's on her way there with her new husband. Also, Aunt Xenia and Uncle Sandro are already there with my six horrid cousins, plus Irina and her husband, Prince Yussupov, who murdered Father Grigory! Although Mama has never forgiven Prince Yussupov for what he did, we all wish we could be there, too.

25 March/7 April 1917

Papa gets upset with the soldiers because they have no military discipline — they don't comb their hair, they don't clean their boots, they leave their jackets unbuttoned. And they don't act like soldiers, either. Yesterday the weather was fine, and one of the soldiers on guard duty carried a gilt chair out of the hall and set it in the sun. There he lounged with his rifle on his knees and his cap shading his eyes while he took a little nap. It did give Papa something to laugh at.

28 March/10 April 1917

No sooner were we all feeling better than Papa and Mama decided we must continue with our studies. And they're to do some of the tutoring! Papa will instruct us in history and geography, and Mama will teach religion. Baroness Buxhoeveden is giving us piano lessons, and the other lady-in-waiting, Countess Hendrikov, will teach art. Monsieur Gilliard is the headmaster and will continue to torture me (this not a mistake for "tutor me") in French, and Mr. Gibbes in English. This will begin next week, after Easter.

I'd hoped we'd be free of studies until we are <u>really</u> free. No such luck.

2/15 April 1917
Easter

Last night after the long midnight service, which we had here in the palace, Papa invited the officers on duty guarding us to join us for our traditional Easter supper. I would have called it a <u>feast</u>, but this was no feast, because of the shortages. There was no sweetened cheese to spread on the kulich, which is supposed to be as light and tender as a cloud but was more like a brick. And there were no flowers.

Mama misses the fresh flowers she always used to have in all her rooms, but the soldiers say flowers are luxuries forbidden to prisoners.

4/17 April 1917

One luxury we do have is Alexei's cinema projector and collection of films. In the evenings Alexei invites anyone he can find to come to his room to watch a <u>performance</u>. Some of the films are really funny, and it keeps Alexei happy.

14/27 April 1917

The snow is nearly gone, and we're sometimes permitted to walk in the park. Mama is always in her wheelchair, and we take turns pushing her. It's awful (I know, I said it again), because everyone stares at us, and sometimes they jeer. Alexei gets upset, because he's used to everybody bowing to Papa. But Papa says we must be polite and friendly, even to those who are impolite and unfriendly to us, that it will pay in the long run. I'm just not sure I can stand the short run.

21 April/4 May 1917

A new officer, Colonel Yevgeny Kobylinsky, has arrived, and Papa says this is good news. The colonel has been wounded twice and was even a patient in one of our hospitals. Papa says he's loyal to us, but that he must do his duty as a soldier and we must not make his job more difficult.

I keep thinking how nice it would be if Mashka's Kolya would be assigned here, but she has heard nothing from him in months and fears the worst.

5/18 May 1917

We're making a vegetable garden in the park. All of us (except Mama, who watches from her wheelchair or her favorite rug) have been digging up the sod and hauling it away. It looks so funny to see M. Gilliard and Mr. Gibbes in their bowler hats, shoveling with the rest of us! Some of the servants are helping, and even a few of the soldiers have pitched in. They must have gotten bored just mocking us.

Tomorrow is Papa's birthday but he says we mustn't fuss. We'll work in the garden again.

22 May/4 June 1917

The seeds are planted, and the weeds haven't yet begun to spring up. We were outside, gazing at our handiwork, when this foolish incident happened: Papa had gone off to saw up some dead trees for firewood for next winter (his latest project), and Alexei began marching around with a toy rifle. Some of the soldiers saw him and thought it was a real gun and started shouting, "They're armed!" and took it away. How stupid they all are.

29 May/11 June 1917

At last a story with a happy ending. Alexei's toy rifle was turned over to Colonel Kobylinsky, who took it apart and has been bringing a piece of it to Alexei each time he comes to visit. He made Alexei promise he would play with it only in his own room. This cheered up Alexei. And when Alexei is happy, Mama is, too. She had been so sad since her birthday four days ago. Now Tatiana can have a nice birthday. Today she is twenty.

1/14 June 1917

Some of the first sprouts have begun to appear in our garden. Radishes, I think, and carrots.

5/18 June 1917

My sixteenth birthday, the year Grandmother promised to take me to Paris. Everyone is trying to be cheerful for my sake. There was even a small cake. I was actually thinking about the necklace that I'm supposed to have, when Mama mentioned it, very quietly. We're sure to be leaving here soon, and we'll need all our jewels — Mama's, my sisters', and mine — to sell later, when we need money. Best gift of all: a new puppy, a spaniel. I'm calling her Jimmy.

17/30 June 1917

We still have no idea when we're leaving, or where we're going. One possibility is England, but that means getting first to a Finnish port, which is very dangerous, because we would have to travel through territory controlled by revolutionary soldiers. Or maybe we'll go to Livadia to be near

Grandmother and our other relatives. We'd love that — even the horrid cousins!

Count Benckendorff says we absolutely must stop talking about going to Livadia, because it could be a bad thing if the soldiers overheard us. Meanwhile, Papa counsels patience: He's sure we will be rescued.

29 June/12 July 1917

Our garden looks terrific! We carry water to it in barrels and pull lots of weeds. I'm getting huge muscles. Jimmy follows me everywhere.

No word yet on our future.

7/20 July 1917

Still no word, but we've begun to pack secretly.

11/24 July 1917

Ratface Kerensky was here an hour ago to talk to Papa. We're leaving soon, but he refused to tell us when or where! All he would say is that we must take plenty of warm clothes. That means we're not going to Livadia. Papa says we have to trust this man.

Now he and Mama are deciding who will go with us. I hate to leave our dear home at Tsarskoe Selo, and I'm also frightened. Where can we be going?

30 July/12 August 1917

Alexei's thirteenth birthday. No party, but a procession of clergy came from the village with a holy icon, and many prayers were said for a safe journey.

31 July/13 August 1917

We're leaving at one o'clock in the morning, and there's much to do to get ready. Papa has instructed Count Benckendorff (who must stay behind because his wife is ill) to distribute the vegetables from our garden and his piles of firewood to the servants who helped with the work. My sisters and Alexei and I made one last trip to our favorite island in the pond. People keep coming up to us and bidding us farewell. We might as well be going to the moon.

3/16 August 1917

On a train

Not to the moon, but to Siberia. Ratface says we'll be quite safe there, which I guess is something. This is not our imperial train, but it's very nice. There's room for servants and for Alexei's dog, Joy, Tatiana's Ortino, and my Jimmy (not that we would consent to leave without them). Eira is staying with Count Benckendorff.

We waited all night and finally left at six in the morning. Yesterday we crossed the Ural Mountains. It's much cooler here.

Colonel Kobylinsky is on the train with us, and there's another train behind this one carrying three hundred soldiers who will guard us. When the train goes through a village, all the blinds are drawn so that no one can see us (and be shocked by the sight of four girls whose hair is still *very* short). There are signs on the cars that say JAPANESE RED CROSS MISSION. Can the people really hate us so much that we must travel in disguise?

———————

5/18 August 1917
On the _Rus_

We left the train yesterday, and now we're going up the Tura River on this little steamer. Once in a while we pass a cluster of cottages. One of these villages was Father Grigory's. Mama reminded us that long ago Father Grigory predicted that she would one day see his village. That made me shudder.

15/28 August 1917
Tobolsk, Siberia

When we arrived last week, the house where we're to stay was a mess — not even any furniture. But Colonel Kobylinsky hired workmen to repair and paint, and now we're nicely settled in. We sisters share one big corner room on the second floor, and it's very cozy. The colonel even got a piano for us. There isn't space for everyone here, so some of our staff stay in a house across the street. We're determined to make the best of this.

21 August/3 September 1917

What a shame. The soldiers got upset when we went across the street to visit our staff — "too much freedom," they said — and so a high wooden fence has been built around our house. We have only a very small (and very muddy) space for exercise.

Good news, though, is that Mr. Gibbes has come out from Petrograd. We were all very glad to see him.

10/23 September 1917

We're allowed to attend early Mass at the church down the street. The soldiers form long lines, and we walk between them. Still, the people of Tobolsk seem friendly and have even sent us gifts of butter and eggs.

We're getting acquainted with the soldiers. They're no happier than we are about being here! Mashka has learned the names of at least a dozen, as well as their wives and children. And Papa and Alexei sometimes go into the guardhouse to play games with the men. They're especially nice to Alexei. Only Mama is completely miserable. She doesn't complain, but I see it on her face.

21 September/4 October 1917

It's already much colder here than at Tsarskoe Selo. By midafternoon the sun has set, and we've turned on the lamps. I try not to think about Livadia!

Papa's only complaint is that he doesn't get his mail regularly. He hasn't seen a newspaper and doesn't know what's happening. I wonder if he still writes in his diary every day. What is there to write when there's nothing to write?!

27 September/10 October 1917

We've settled into a routine not much different from the one at Tsarskoe Selo, at least for us children. Papa no longer has endless meetings, but we still have endless classes, starting at nine o'clock. Mama is constantly busy sewing our clothes, especially mine. I'm ashamed to say why: Olga and Tatiana get thinner and thinner, but I'm doing the opposite. Also, she's knitting stockings for Alexei because we know that the winter is going to be fiercely cold.

9/22 October 1917

Mama has a letter from Anya. She's been released from the fortress, thank God. She says it was terrible and she didn't think she'd survive. I hope Anya will be able to find a way to get us out of here.

2/15 November 1917

Papa finally got some news, and it truly shocked him. Kerensky, the one I call Ratface, is out of power, and the Provisional Government has been overthrown by a revolutionary group called the Bolsheviks. Papa says they want the government to be run by the workers! But one of their leaders, Vladimir Ilyitch Lenin, is a traitor who betrayed Russia for his own gain. For the first time, Papa is sorry he abdicated, which he did for the good of the Russian people, if the result is that Russia has fallen into the hands of evil men.

3/16 November 1917

Olga's birthday. A dismal day.

———•◆•———

24 November/7 December 1917

Our room has turned into an icebox, and we wear layer upon layer of clothing to keep warm. Jimmy sleeps on my feet, which helps. But poor Ortino shivers all the time.

Worse than being cold, we are absolutely bored to tears. We can go nowhere, and hardly anyone can come here. We get no exercise but marching up and down behind Papa in the little enclosure. The only thing that's keeping us busy is making Christmas presents for the servants and Mama's ladies and Papa's suite. I'm in charge of painting ribbons to use as bookmarks, and my sisters knit waistcoats until their fingers ache.

26 November/9 December 1917

Ortino is ill. Tatiana is frantic.

30 November/13 December 1917

Mr. Gibbes and M. Gilliard have come up with a grand idea: We're forming a little theater company, and we're planning to put on plays for whomever we can convince to be our audience. Mama has agreed to write our programs, and Papa is cast in the title role of our first production, Chekhov's *The Bear*. (What a coincidence that the play I wrote on the *Standart* had the same title.)

The most enthusiastic of our actors is Alexei, who loves the idea of putting on a false beard and speaking in a growl. (His voice has begun to change, but it tends to squeak when he least wants it to. Too funny, but we dare not laugh.)

1/14 December 1917

Ortino seemed to be improving but this morning took a turn for the worse. This evening he died. Tatiana weeps.

25 December 1917/7 January 1918

The day started off the way Christmas <u>should</u>, and then something happened that ruined everything. As usual we went to the little church on the far side of the public garden for Mass, and at the end of the service the priest said a prayer for the health and long life of the imperial family. Huge mistake! That prayer had been dropped from the Mass after Papa's abdication, and the soldiers got angry when they heard it. So we've been told that's the last time we'll be allowed to attend the little church. From now on we must have our services here in the house. As if that wasn't bad enough, we're going to have guards <u>inside</u> the house, as well as outside.

8/21 January 1918

We're building a snow mountain, like the ones we always had at Tsarskoe Selo. We've been working like slaves, shoveling tons of snow and carrying gallons of water from the kitchen to pour on the mountain to make it icy. It's so cold that the water nearly freezes in the bucket before we can get it to the top!

20 January/2 February 1918

Our mountain is finished, and my sisters and I have made up all kinds of races and games that always seem to end up with me facedown in the snow.

30 January/12 February 1918

A new problem: money. The soldiers are not being paid, and they're upset and angry, as though it were our fault! Also, when the cook tries to shop for food, the merchants won't give him credit. No one speaks to <u>me</u> about this, of course, but I hear the talk.

12/25 February 1918

We've been notified that we're to be put on soldier's rations, beginning next week. The first items to go will be butter and coffee. We won't miss butter too much, because it's nearly time for Lent, and all of us prefer tea to coffee, anyway. One of our nicest servants, Sonia Petrovna Izvolsky, has promised to smuggle us eggs for Alexei from her henhouse.

But Papa has also decided that we must dismiss some of our servants. This will be hard because many of them brought their families here to Tobolsk, and now these loyal servants will have no way to earn a living. I hope he doesn't dismiss Sonia.

22 February/7 March 1918

I'm so furious, I could scream. Our snow mountain has been destroyed by soldiers with picks, for a very stupid reason.

A regiment of soldiers we'd grown fond of were leaving (we knew not only their names but also their wives and children), and Papa and Alexei climbed to the top of the hill to salute them. Someone saw them and announced that it was "dangerous." So our mountain is no more. Alexei stared at the wreckers silently, with big, sunken eyes.

4/17 March 1918

It's Butterweek, for everyone but us. We're stuck in this old house, half frozen, while beneath the windows we can hear the *troikas* dashing by, pulling sleighs with their little bells jingling. People out there are having fun, and we're in here covered in gloom.

Papa tells us not to be gloomy, that we have many loyal friends who will certainly find a way to rescue us. But <u>when</u>?

Mama believes God will send us help at Easter, the time of the Resurrection.

6/19 March 1918

Papa has just received terrible news: Two weeks ago the Bolshevik government led by Vladimir Ilyitch Lenin signed a peace treaty with the Germans. It's called the Treaty of Brest-Litovsk, and the Bolsheviks agreed to surrender Poland, Ukraine, the Crimea (Livadia!), and other Russian territory. Papa is completely overwhelmed with grief. It's as though the country he loves so much has died. I don't know what to do to console him.

12/25 March 1918

A terrible accident. Alexei, his snow mountain destroyed, took it into his head to ride his sled <u>down the stairs</u> inside the house. He fell and hurt himself in the groin. Now he's bleeding inside and is in horrible pain. I can hear his screams from my room. He says he wants to die. I just can't bear it.

17/30 March 1918

Alexei is a little better. The pain is less, although he still can't walk. We all take turns staying with him, reading to him, playing cards.

New troops are arriving every day. I don't know what this means. I thought the war was over. Why are all these soldiers here?

———•◦•———

22 March/4 April 1918

Spring does come, even in Siberia. It would be so much more enjoyable if we could have some real exercise. For some reason I've been dreaming about riding a horse.

3/16 April 1918

All sorts of rumors are buzzing that someone very important is coming here from Moscow. Papa thinks it might even be Leon Trotsky, another Bolshevik leader. He says Trotsky is just as bad as Lenin.

9/22 April 1918

Our important visitor is here — not Leon Trotsky, but Commissar Vassily Yakovlev, sent by Vladimir Lenin. The commissar arrived at the head of 150 horsemen, and he brought a private telegraph operator so that he can send wires directly to the Kremlin in Moscow. (It's now the capital, not Petrograd.) The commissar is very polite to Mama, bows to Papa, and so on, and they all seem to like each other. We're not sure why he is here. There is even a rumor that he's really come to rescue us. Baroness Buxhoeveden thinks we'll go to Norway, but I heard Dr. Botkin whispering something about Japan. How exciting that would be!

12/25 April 1918

So far we've been wrong about everything. The reason Commissar Yakovlev is here is to take Papa away, to Moscow for trial. (But he has not committed any crime!) At first we thought we would all go with him. But Alexei is worse again, very thin and in great pain, much too ill to make a long journey. I won't describe the tearful scene that followed, but here's what was decided: Mama will go with Papa, and take Mashka with her! The rest of us will stay here until we find out what's next.

We all agreed, as awful as it is, because Olga is in very low spirits, and Tatiana is the one who must look after Alexei. I'm to stay here because, as Mama and my sisters decided, "Anastasia is too young."

Too young! That made me feel even worse, but I said nothing because it's all too horrible, anyway. We've never been separated, except when Alexei was with Papa at *Stavka*, and I don't know how we'll bear it.

I am nearly seventeen years old — hardly a child. Perhaps this is the time to prove to my parents that I am no longer a *shvibzik*, an imp, but a person who has earned their confidence.

13/26 April 1918

They're gone. They left in a string of filthy peasant carts this morning before it was light. Mama was riding on a bed of straw, with Dr. Botkin's fur cloak over her. The doctor and several others went with them.

Olga, Tatiana, Alexei, and I sit and stare at each other. We dare not wonder aloud when we will see them again.

17/30 April 1918

A telegram from Mama: They're in a place called Ekaterinburg. This is a total surprise to us, because we were told they were going to Moscow. We can't imagine what's going to happen.

———◆———

22 *April/5 May 1918*

Easter, but no celebration — just four of us with our servants, praying together. Sonia brought us four eggs and some tasty cheese, which we devoured. She's so kind!

23 *April/6 May 1918*

A letter from Mama, at last, describing their long journey. We'll be sent for soon, she says, and in the meantime we're to "dispose of the medicines as has been agreed." This was the code we agreed upon just before they left. All the jewels we brought with us from Tsarskoe Selo are to be hidden in our clothing so that they won't be found when we go to Ekaterinburg. Who would have guessed that I would someday be a jewel smuggler!

26 *April/9 May 1918*

Tatiana is in charge: With Sonia and two of the servants we trust most, we're busy sewing the jewels into our clothing. Sonia is very clever. She's covered some of the jewels with cloth, to look like buttons. Others are stitched into our corsets. Alexei keeps watch with our two dogs so that we aren't surprised by the wrong persons.

28 April/11 May 1918

Colonel Kobylinsky has been relieved of his position. We've come to know him after a long year, and I was a little sorry to see him go. I was even sorrier when I met his replacement, a bully named Rodionov, chief officer of the Red Guards, who's to take us to Ekaterinburg as soon as Alexei is well enough to travel. He's an awful person! I was waving out the window to Gleb Botkin, and Rodionov threatened to shoot anyone who waves back to us. Such a beast.

6/19 May 1918

We leave tomorrow, on the river steamer *Rus* that brought us here. Then we'll take a train to Ekaterinburg. All is ready — even the dogs. The "medicines" have all been "disposed of." I can hardly wait to see Mama and Papa and Mashka again.

I nearly forgot: This is Papa's fiftieth birthday.

Later

Tatiana has given me something new to worry about. She asked me what I'm planning to do with this diary, and if I've written things in it that I don't want the guards to read — about hiding the jewels, for instance. I confessed that I had.

"Then you must burn it," she said. "You can't take it with you."

I know she's right. But this diary has been my friend for a long time, and I can't bear to destroy it.

So this is what I've decided: I'll entrust this diary to Sonia, who lives here in Tobolsk and has been kind to me, and ask her to keep it safe for me. Then, when we're free, I'll write to her from England or Japan or wherever we're going, and ask her to send it to me.

And so, farewell to you, dear diary. Until we meet again.

Anastasia Nichalaievna Romanov

Epilogue

On May 20, 1918, Anastasia, Tatiana, Olga, and Alexei, accompanied by Sailor Nagorny, M. Gilliard, Mr. Gibbes, and other loyal members of the family's staff, left Tobolsk. Some of the staff were immediately arrested and sent to prison. Others, including the two tutors, were released when they arrived in Ekaterinburg and ordered to leave the city.

The sisters, Alexei, and their parents had a joyous reunion in Ekaterinburg. They went to stay at a house prepared for them, ominously named "the House of Special Purpose." A dozen people shared five rooms, but they were happy to be together again.

Life at the House of Special Purpose was far from pleasant. The head of the guards, Alexander Avdeyev, was a drunken boor who swore and told lewd jokes in the presence of the tsaritsa and the grand duchesses. The young women were not allowed to use the lavatory unless they were escorted by soldiers.

Yet somehow their life went on. It was spring, and they had their daily walks in the garden. Alexei, still bedridden much of the time, played with a model ship, and his mother and sisters read, knitted, and embroidered. The dogs entertained them. Sometimes in the evenings the family sang hymns to drown out the singing of the drunken soldiers.

The imperial family quickly established a routine, much as they always had, rising at eight for morning prayers, followed by breakfast, and a main meal at two o'clock. But their diet had certainly changed: Breakfast was black bread and tea, and lunch was soup and some kind of meat served on a table without either linen or silverware. Avdeyev and the other soldiers watched them eat and sometimes stuck their hands in the stewpot to seize a piece of meat. "You've had enough, you idle rich," the Romanovs were told.

Sailor Navgorny once tried to stop a soldier from stealing a gold chain belonging to Alexei. Navgorny was promptly arrested; four days later he was shot. Now it was the tsar's task to carry his son outside, for after his accident with the sled on the stairs at Tobolsk, the tsarevitch did not walk again.

The days stretched into weeks. Summer came. Anastasia had her seventeenth birthday. There wasn't much to celebrate, but the family still did not give up hope of rescue.

On July 4, Avdeyev and his drunken soldiers were replaced by the Secret Police. Their leader, Yakov Yurovsky, was not as boorish and insulting as his predecessor, but he was cold and apparently heartless. Determinedly brave until now, the family became afraid. They learned that the White Army, troops opposed to the Red Army of the Bolsheviks, were approaching Ekaterinburg. This might have seemed like good news, but Nicholas and Alexandra knew that if the city fell to the White Army, the Bolsheviks would have the Romanovs shot before they could be rescued.

Ten days later, the family sensed a change in the behavior of their captors. Something was about to happen.

Tuesday, July 16, passed like any other day. Late in the afternoon, Tsar Nicholas and the four grand duchesses went for a walk in the garden. By 10:30, the family had all gone to bed. Shortly after midnight on July 17, the head of the Secret Police woke them and ordered them to dress and go downstairs. They did as they were told. Anastasia carried her dog, Jimmy. The tsar carried Alexei, and someone else brought Alexei's spaniel, Joy. The guards crowded them into a basement room with Dr. Botkin and some of the family's servants. Nicholas asked for chairs for Alexandra and Alexei. The chairs were brought.

Eleven executioners entered. The shooting began.

By early morning, all were dead — Nicholas, Alexandra, Olga, Tatiana, Marie, Anastasia, Alexei, their friends, and their servants. The bodies were carted away and destroyed with acid so that the remains would not be found.

A total of nineteen members of the Romanov family, including Grand Duchess Elizabeth, Anastasia's aunt Ella, were murdered by the Bolsheviks in 1918. A few survived; one was Anastasia's grandmother, Dowager Empress Marie Feodorovna, who in the spring of 1919 left Russia by ship for England. She never returned. The dowager empress died in 1928.

But the story of this tragic family refused to die. For years a myth persisted that Anastasia somehow managed to survive the executioners' bullets and bayonets (the jewels sewn into the women's corsets were believed to have caused some of the bullets to bounce off) and that she had escaped from the House of Special Purpose and from Russia itself. During the 1920s several young women came forward, each claiming to be the lost grand duchess. (There were rumors that the imperial family had hidden vast amounts of wealth in Europe, money that might be claimed by a survivor.) A woman named Anna Anderson succeeded in convincing many people that she was indeed Anastasia Nicholaievna Romanov. Anna Anderson died in the 1960s, before DNA testing could prove or disprove her claim. Books and movies about Anastasia's miraculous survival have helped keep the myth alive.

Eventually, though, remains of the victims were discovered. Extensive testing has proved that they are those of the Romanovs and their servants. Still, not all of the imperial family has been accounted for: Alexei and one of the grand duchesses is missing. Scientists disagree about whether the missing girl is Marie or Anastasia. On July 17, 1998, the eightieth anniversary of their assassination, the remains of the Romanovs were finally buried in the Cathedral of Sts. Peter and Paul in St. Petersburg, where nearly every Russian tsar and tsaritsa since the time of Peter the Great has been laid to rest.

Life in Russia
in 1914

Historical Note

The Russia ruled by Nicholas II was enormous, the largest country in the world, extending from the Arctic Ocean on the north to the Black Sea on the south, from the Baltic Sea on the west to the Pacific Ocean on the east. Across this vast continent were scattered the tsar's 150 million subjects, from poor, illiterate peasants to noble families of great wealth.

The word *tsar* (sometimes spelled *czar*) means "emperor" and comes from Caesar, the title given to the emperors of ancient Rome. The tsar's power over rich and poor alike was absolute. The first Russian prince to call himself tsar of Russia was a man who later became known as Ivan the Terrible. He ruled as tsar from 1547 to 1584.

Needing a wife, Ivan summoned two thousand young women to be paraded past him. Out of them he chose a girl from a wealthy family in Moscow. Her name was Anastasia Romanov. Not long after they married, Anastasia died, and Ivan was so overcome with grief that he went mad. He was known to carry an iron staff, which he used to spear anyone who happened to anger him. Sixty thousand people were tortured to death while he watched, and he burned many villages to the ground. In a fit of rage, he fatally stabbed his favorite son.

The period following Ivan's death was filled with confusion. Many people claimed the throne. Finally, the national assembly decided to elect a new tsar. The only candidate on whom they could agree was Ivan's grand-nephew, a sixteen-year-old boy named Michael Romanov. In 1613, Michael became the founder of the Romanov dynasty.

Several generations later, in 1682, Peter I came to power. Nearly seven feet tall, he was known as Peter the Great and was a powerful man in many ways. He wanted to modernize Russia by opening the country to progressive European ideas. With this in mind, he built St. Petersburg, designed to be a European-style city. The Great Palace at Peterhof was built in imitation of Versailles in France.

Peter the Great also had a bad side: He threatened to cut off the head of anyone caught sleeping with his boots on, because that showed the person was backward, not interested in modernizing Russia. Sometimes he pulled out the teeth of subjects who displeased him!

Peter's grandson, Peter III, later married a German princess named Sophie, who changed her name to Catherine and forced her husband to abdicate so that she could rule. Under Catherine II, called Catherine the Great, Russia became a major world power in the eighteenth century. But the tsars were still harsh, and the peasants remained trapped in lives of wretched poverty while the aristocrats accumulated more and more wealth.

Over the next century, attempts were made to bring reforms to Russia that would improve the lot of ordinary citizens. But after a terrorist's bomb killed Tsar Alexander II in 1881, his successor, Alexander III, began a reign that undid many of the reforms. This was the father of Nicholas, who would become Russia's next, and last, tsar in 1894.

When Alexander III died of kidney disease, Nicholas was twenty-six years old and completely unprepared to rule. He had neither the training, the talent, nor the desire to assume such responsibility, yet he believed that he was ordained by God to fulfill his destiny. In time both destiny and responsibility overwhelmed him.

Soon after his father's unexpected death, Nicholas married a German princess, Alix Victoria Helena Louise Beatrice, princess of Hesse-Darmstadt, granddaughter of Queen Victoria of England. Following a year of mourning, the couple was crowned in a five-hour ceremony in Assumption Cathedral on May 14 (May 26), 1896. The day after the coronation, a half million people rushed to a nearby park to celebrate. Fanned by rumors of shortages of food and drink, a panic swept through the crowd. Hundreds died in the ensuing mayhem. The decision of the imperial couple to go ahead with the coronation ball despite the tragedy was remembered years later as a sign of the heartlessness of "Bloody Nicholas" and "the German woman."

Four grand duchesses were born to the imperial couple before there was an heir at last — Alexei Nicholaievitch. From his birth there were deep concerns about the health of the tsarevitch. Like many of Queen Victoria's descendants, Alexei had inherited hemophilia, a genetic disease that affects chiefly males, passed on by mothers to their sons. Hemophiliacs have no clotting factor in their blood, meaning that even a minor injury can result in blood pooling in the joints and internal organs, causing terrible pain, crippling, swelling, and death. Not much could be done medically for Alexei at that time. His worried parents did their best to protect him from injury and, at the same time, keep his serious condition a secret from the Russian people.

It was during one of Alexei's early attacks that Father Grigory, known as Rasputin, began to grow in influence in the imperial family. Born Grigory Efimovitch, the son of a peasant in a Siberian village, he was nicknamed Rasputin (meaning "dissolute") by his neighbors for his wanton behavior. He left his wife and children and moved to St. Petersburg, where he passed himself off as a holy man.

Anya Vyrubova first made his acquaintance and, impressed by his mystical powers, introduced him to Tsaritsa Alexandra. Although the tsaritsa regarded Father Grigory as a miracle worker because Alexei's condition always improved after the holy man had spoken to him, it is more likely that Rasputin used a kind of hypnosis to calm the suffering child and his hysterical mother. Soon Alexandra began to depend on Father Grigory for advice of all kinds.

The tsaritsa, who took the name Alexandra when she converted to the Russian Orthodox faith before her coronation, was not a popular figure. Unlike her mother-in-law, the Dowager Empress Marie Feodorovna, Alexandra was not a sociable person and disliked the grand balls and public appearances that were a vital part of Russian court society. Tsarevitch Alexei's illness gave Alexandra more cause to withdraw, adding to the public's disapproval.

During those same years, the discontent of the Russian people grew stronger. In 1904, lured by Kaiser Wilhelm of Germany, his wife's cousin, the tsar had allowed Russia to become involved in a war against Japan.

Most of Russia's ships were sunk in a single day, and she

lost the war. In January 1905, unarmed workers marched to the tsar's Winter Palace in St. Petersburg to demand reforms. Troops fired on the peaceful crowd, and hundreds of marchers were killed or wounded. The revolutionary movement gained strength, and in October 1905, a strike paralyzed the country. Under pressure, Tsar Nicholas allowed the formation of the Duma, an elected assembly, with the ability to pass on proposed laws. But the tsar wasn't used to the idea of sharing power, and he dissolved the Duma, later reinstating it.

Grand Duchess Anastasia was born into an exotic world of almost unlimited wealth and privilege that cushioned her and her sisters and brother from harsh reality. It was not until Russia entered World War I that their bubble burst and the outside world intruded. As Russia's wartime losses mounted, and hunger and privation became widespread, dislike of the Romanovs intensified accordingly. Nicholas's misguided attempts to take over the leadership of the military, leaving his wife to manage the affairs of a vast and complex country, further weakened Russia.

In March 1917, the people revolted, staging violent riots and strikes. Realizing he no longer had support, Tsar Nicholas abdicated his throne; the Duma set up what was named the Provisional Government. Eight months later, Bolshevik revolutionaries overthrew the Provisional Government and formed a new government headed by Vladimir Lenin. In 1918, the Bolsheviks moved the capital from Petrograd to Moscow. It was under orders from the Bolshevik revolutionaries that the tsar and his family were murdered. Their deep love of Russia and its people failed to save them.

The Bolsheviks later became the Communist Party that took over Russia and other republics to form the Soviet Union. Until 1991, when it broke apart, the Soviet Union was the world's most powerful Communist country.

Today, history views Alexandra as a lonely, frightened woman who listened to the wrong advice: Rasputin's. Nicholas is remembered as a weak ruler, a kindly man who also listened to bad advice: his wife's. And we are left to wonder what kind of woman Anastasia would have become had her life not ended so early and so tragically.

The Romanov Family Tree

Alice
1843–1878

=

Louis IV
Grand Duke of Hesse
1837–1892

Victoria
1863–1950

**Elizabeth
(Ella)**
1864–1918

Irene
1866–1953

**Ernst
(Ernie)**
1868–1937

= **Louis of
Battenberg**
1854–1921

= **Sergei**
1857–1905

= **Henry
of Prussia**
1862–1929

= **Victoria
Melita
of Saxe-
Coburg**
1876–1936

Alice
1885–1969

Waldemar
1889–1945

**Louis (Earl
Mountbatten
of Burma)**
1900–1979

Sigismund
1896–1978

Henry
1900–1904

Frederick
1870–1873

Mary
1874–1878

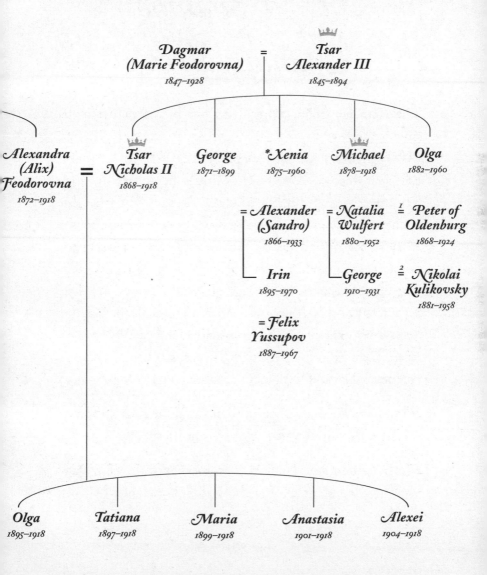

	Dagmar *(Marie Feodorovna)* *1847–1928*	=	👑 **Tsar** **Alexander III** *1845–1894*		

Alexandra
(Alix)
Feodorovna
1872–1918

=

👑
Tsar
Nicholas II
1868–1918

George
1871–1899

*Xenia
1875–1960

👑
Michael
1878–1918

Olga
1882–1960

= **Alexander**
(Sandro)
1866–1933

= **Natalia**
Wulfert
1880–1952

$\overset{1}{=}$ **Peter of**
Oldenburg
1868–1924

└ **Irin**
1895–1970

└ **George**
1910–1931

$\overset{2}{=}$ **Nikolai**
Kulikovsky
1881–1958

= **Felix**
Yussupov
1887–1967

Olga
1895–1918

Tatiana
1897–1918

Maria
1899–1918

Anastasia
1901–1918

Alexei
1904–1918

*Xenia and Sandro had six other children.

The Romanov Family Tree

The Romanov ruling family was one of the richest of its time in lands and wealth. The dynasty began with Mikhail (Michael) Feodorovitch Romanov (1596–1645), a young aristocrat who was elected tsar of Russia on January 13, 1613. The dynasty ended with Michael Romanov's descendant Nicholas II, who linked together two powerful royal houses when he married a German princess, Alexandra (Alix) Feodorovna, the granddaughter of Queen Victoria of England. The chart illustrates the lineage of the Romanovs and their royal relatives through marriage beginning with the last tsar and tsaritsa's parents. The crown symbol indicates those who ruled. Double lines represent marriages; single lines indicate parentage. Dates of birth and death are noted.

Alexander III: The father of Nicholas II, he ruled as tsar of Russia for thirteen years until his death in 1894.

Marie Feodorovna: Nicholas's mother, born Princess Dagmar (called Minnie), was the youngest daughter of King

Christian IX of Denmark and his queen, Louise of Hesse-Cassel.

Nicholas II: He was the eldest of the five children of Tsar Alexander III and Empress Marie Feodorovna. Born on May 6 (May 19), 1868, he was crowned tsar on May 14 (May 26), 1896. Nicholas II was assassinated with his wife and children in the early hours of July 17, 1918, in the Impatiev House in Ekaterinburg (now Sverdlovsk) in the Urals of western Russia.

Alexandra Feodorovna: Was born Alix Victoria Helena Louise Beatrice, Princess of Hesse on May 25 (June 7), 1872. She was the sixth child of Queen Victoria's daughter, Alice, and Ludwig (Louis) of Hesse-Darmstadt, then one of the German states. She converted to the Russian Orthodox faith and became Alexandra. She married Nicholas II on November 14 (November 26), 1894, in the chapel of the Winter Palace.

Children of Tsar Nicholas II and Tsaritsa Alexandra:

Grand Duchess Olga Nicholaievna: The eldest daughter of Nicholas and Alexandra, she was born on November 3 (November 16), 1895.

Grand Duchess Tatiana Nicholaievna: The second daughter of Nicholas and Alexandra, born on May 29 (June 11), 1897. She was her mother's favorite companion.

Grand Duchess Maria Nicholaievna: Born June 14 (June 27), 1899, she was known as Marie or Mashka.

Grand Duchess Anastasia Nicholaievna: She was born June 5 (June 18), 1901, and throughout her life was the favorite of her grandmother Marie Feodorovna.

Alexis Nicholaievitch: Known as Alexei, the tsarevitch was born on July 30 (August 12), 1904. Called Baby and Sunbeam by his parents, just weeks after his birth, they realized he had hemophilia, a blood disorder transmitted only to sons from a mother who has inherited the gene. The family kept this a secret as much as possible.

An undated photograph of Grand Duchess Anastasia Romanov, youngest daughter of Tsar Nicholas II.

*An undated photograph of Russia's last tsar, Nicholas II, and
Alexandra Feodorovna at the time of their engagement.*

Tsar Nicholas II and the imperial family. From top row: Olga, Tatiana, Maria, the tsaritsa, the tsar, Anastasia, and Alexei.

Tsar Nicholas II and the tsarevitch, Alexei.

A very rare and undated photograph of the eerie-looking Grigory Efimovitch Rasputin, trusted counselor to Tsaritsa Alexandra.

An aerial view of the expansive 800-acre compound Tsarskoe Selo (the Tsar's Village) near St. Petersburg. On site are the great and lavish Catherine Palace (named after Catherine I) and the smaller, less grandiose Alexander Palace (100 rooms), which was the main residence of the Romanov family and Nicholas's birthplace. The sprawling grounds included immaculately manicured lawns, gardens with elaborate fountains and statues, a man-made lake, and a park.

Peterhof Palace was built by Tsar Peter the Great, in imitation of the Palace of Versailles in France.

A view of the Winter Palace, former home of Russian emperors, including the imperial family of Tsar Nicholas II. Built between 1754 and 1762, the palace, where the wedding of Nicholas II and Alexandra took place, is now part of the State Hermitage Museum in St. Petersburg.

Interior view of the tsar's library in the Winter Palace.

Livadia in the Crimea overlooks the Black Sea. The favorite summer home of the Romanov family was built by Nicholas and Alexandra soon after their marriage.

Olga and Tatiana with tutor, Pierre Gilliard, on the terrace of Livadia, circa 1910.

Tsar Nicholas II and the imperial family aboard the luxurious royal yacht Standart, *pictured above.*

Thousands of soldiers marched off to the war traveling down this popular shopping boulevard, Nevsky Prospect, in St. Petersburg. Pictured circa 1900.

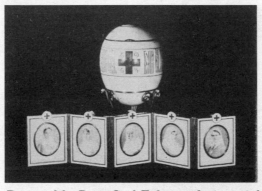

Designed by Peter Carl Fabergé, the imperial Easter egg of 1915, made of white enamel with a red cross, honors the Romanov women who became war nurses. Their photographs, shown here, fit inside the egg. Pictured left to right: the tsar's sister Olga, his daughters Olga and Tatiana, Tsaritsa Alexandra, and the tsar's first cousin Marie Pavlovna.

Alexei with his spaniel, Joy, on a visit to the imperial army in the field, photographed 1917.

Tsar Nicholas II and Alexei at the front in 1916.

The tsar, the tsaritsa, and their children working in the garden while imprisoned at Tsarskoe Selo.

Tsar Nicholas under guard by Russian soldiers at Tsarskoe Selo, photographed August 19, 1917.

Prisoners in exile. Anastasia, with her father, sisters, and brother, sits on the roof of their prison house in Tobolsk, Siberia.

Ipatiev House, "the House of Special Purpose," in Sverdlovsk (formerly Ekaterinburg) where Tsar Nicholas II and his family were executed on July 17, 1918.

Russian president Boris Yeltsin and wife before the tomb with the remains of Tsar Nicholas II at the burial ceremony in the Cathedral of Sts. Peter and Paul, July 1998.

About the Russian Language

Russian is a Slavic language spoken today by over 150 million people. The Russian alphabet, called the Cyrillic alphabet, has thirty-three letters based largely on the Greek alphabet. When Russian is translated into English, letters from the Roman alphabet are substituted for the sound of the Cyrillic letters, and not all translators make the same substitutions. This is why *tsar* is sometimes written as *czar*. Names also appear with different spellings: *Alexei* is sometimes written as *Aleksey*, and *Anya* as *Annia*.

In the Romanovs' time, Russians properly addressed one another by their first, or given name, followed by the patronymic, the name of their father, with a feminine or masculine ending added. That's why Anastasia was properly called *Anastasia Nicholaievna* (*Anastasia*, daughter of *Nicholas*), and her brother was *Alexei Nicholaievitch* (*Alexei*, son of *Nicholas*).

About the Russian Calendar

The calendar used in Anastasia's time, called the Julian calendar, was significantly different from the Gregorian calendar that was in use in most other parts of the world. The Julian calendar, named for Julius Caesar, had been in use for more than 1,500 years. The Julian year was 365 days and 6 hours — 11 minutes and 14 seconds longer than the time Earth actually takes to revolve around the sun. Over the years those minutes and seconds added up, so by A.D. 1580 the vernal (spring) equinox was actually occurring ten days later than the date shown on the calendar.

Taking the advice of astronomers, Pope Gregory XIII corrected the difference by dropping ten days and making some adjustments to the leap year with its additional day in February. In 1582, the Pope's Gregorian calendar was adopted by most Roman Catholic countries in Europe. German states kept the old calendar until 1700, and Great

Britain and the American colonies did not change until 1752. Russia and Turkey were the last to accept the new calendar, in 1918.

During Anastasia's time, the difference between the old Julian calendar and the new Gregorian calendar had increased to thirteen days. Her parents and many other educated Russians sometimes used both systems, perhaps dating a letter written to a relative in England "23 October/5 November," meaning that the letter was being written according to the "Old Style" Russian calendar on October 23, but that on the Englishman's calendar the date was November 5.

The calendar of Christian feast and fast days was also affected. Christmas was celebrated on December 25 according to the Russian calendar, but that date was thirteen days later than Christmas in Germany, France, and the United States, where it was already January 7 of the following year. Easter is more complicated, because the date changes every year according to ancient formulas. But the Russian Orthodox Church and the Greek Orthodox Church use a formula that is different from the formula used by Western Christian churches. As a result, the Russian Orthodox date of Easter and other holy days related to it can vary as much as a few weeks from the date observed in the rest of the world.

Anastasia's diary uses both Old Style and New Style dates, as her mother did in hers.

Glossary of Characters

Anastasia's Family:

Nicholas Alexandrovitch Romanov — tsar; Anastasia's father

Alexandra Feodorovna Romanov — tsaritsa; Anastasia's mother

Olga
Tatiana
Maria (Marie, Mashka) } grand duchesses; Anastasia's sisters

Alexei — tsarevitch; Anastasia's brother

Marie Feodorovna Romanov — tsar's mother; Anastasia's grandmother

Olga Alexandrovna (Aunt Olga) — tsar's sister

Xenia Alexandrovna (Aunt Xenia) — tsar's sister

Alexander Mikhailovitch (Uncle Sandro) — Aunt Xenia's husband and tsar's cousin

Irina, Andrew, Theodore, Dmitri, Vassily, Rostislav, Nikita — children of Xenia and Sandro; Anastasia's cousins

Michael Alexandrovitch Romanov (Uncle Misha) — tsar's
brother

Nicholas Nicholaievitch Romanov — tsar's cousin;
commander-in-chief of the armies

George Mikhailovitch Romanov — tsar's cousin; husband of Queen Marie of Greece; father of Nina; Uncle
Sandro's brother

Elizabeth of Hesse (Aunt Ella) — tsaritsa's sister

Ernst Ludwig of Hes`se (Uncle Erni) — tsaritsa's brother

Wilhelm II, Kaiser (Cousin Willy) — tsaritsa's cousin

FRIENDS OF THE ROMANOVS:

Father Grigory (Rasputin) — holy man; adviser to
tsaritsa

Anya Vyrubova — tsaritsa's close friend

Lili Dehn — tsaritsa's close friend

Baroness Buxhoeveden ⎫
Countess Hendrikov ⎬ members of the
Count Benckendorff ⎪ imperial suite
Prince Dolgoruky ⎭

Dr. Botkin — family physician

Gleb Botkin — his son; Anastasia's friend

Dr. Derevenko — Alexei's physician

Emir of Bokhara — exotic visitor

Crown Prince Carol of Romania — Olga's suitor
King Ferdinand — his father
Queen Marie — his mother
Nicholas Dmitrievitch Demekov (Kolya) — Mashka's friend
*Lieutenant Boris — Anastasia's dancing partner
*Mrs. Phelps — English visitor
*Officer Saltikov — Tatiana's dancing partner

MEMBERS OF THE HOUSEHOLD, SERVANTS, OTHERS:
Shura — Anastasia's nurse-governess
Monsieur Gilliard
Mr. Gibbes } children's tutors
Professor Petrov
Sailor Derevenko — Alexei's sailor-guardian
Sailor Nagorny — Alexei's sailor-guardian
Father Vasilev — family priest
Jim — American door attendant
Carl Fabergé — jeweler; creator of Easter eggs
Madame Gheringer — supplier of scarves, gloves, etc.
*Dunyasha — Olga's maid
*Natasha — Dunyasha's daughter

*Vladya — Natasha's fiancé
*Miss Kropotkin — children's music teacher
*Lutka — servant
*Sonia Petrovna Izvolsky — servant
*Kremikov — court photographer

MILITARY AND POLITICAL OFFICIALS:

General Kornilov — respected leader who informed the tsaritsa of arrest

Alexander Kerensky — Minister of Justice

Colonel Yevgeny Kobylinsky — officer in charge of prisoners

Commissar Rodionov — officer who replaced Kobylinsky

Commissar Vassily Yakovlev — representative of Bolshevik government in Tobolsk

Commandant Avdeyev — head of guards at Ekaterinburg

Commandant Yurovsky — head of Secret Police

OTHER IMPORTANT FIGURES:

Mathilde Kschessinska — *prima ballerina assoluta* of the Imperial Ballet

Vladimir Ilyitch Lenin — Bolshevik leader

Leon Trotsky — Bolshevik leader

Prince Felix Yussupov — husband of the tsar's niece, Irina; assassin of Rasputin

Family Pets:
Vanka — Alexei's donkey
Eira — tsaritsa's Scottish terrier
Ortino — Tatiana's French bulldog
Joy — Alexei's spaniel
Jimmy — Anastasia's spaniel

About the Author

Long ago, Carolyn Meyer fell in love with the story of Anastasia Romanov, the daughter of the last tsar of Russia. "The movies made her life seem so romantic, like a fairy tale. Years ago I saw a movie starring Ingrid Bergman as Anastasia. Later, I saw the animated version of the story. Those movies always made it seem as though everything turned out beautifully for Anastasia. I was broken-hearted when I found out the truth.

"Anastasia was born in this century. It was hard for me to imagine a girl born about the same time as my mother living a life of such incredible wealth and privilege. I loved looking at photographs of the Romanovs' palaces and their enormous yacht and luxurious train. And those marvelous Fabergé Easter eggs! But I hated reading about what really happened to the Grand Duchess Anastasia and her family—the part you don't see in the movies. The tragedy made me want to weep—and in fact I did, as I wrote the final pages."

Carolyn Meyer is the acclaimed author of nearly sixty books for middle school and young adult readers. Among her many award-winning novels are *Victoria Rebels*;

Cleopatra Confesses; *Marie, Dancing*, a Book Sense Pick; and *Mary, Bloody Mary*, an ABA's Pick of the Lists, an NCSS-CBC Notable Children's Trade Book in the Field of Social Studies, and an ALA Best Book for Young Adults. She lives in Albuquerque, New Mexico, and you can visit her at www.ReadCarolyn.com.

Acknowledgments

Grateful acknowledgment is made for permission to use the following:

Cover art by Mélanie Delon.

Filigree on front and back cover by albumkoretsky/Shutterstock.

Crown appearing on spine and throughout interiors, ibid.

Page 187: Anastasia, Library of Congress.

Page 188: Tsar Nicholas II and Alexandra, Culver Pictures.

Page 189 (top): The imperial family, Library of Congress.

Page 189 (bottom): Tsar Nicholas II with his son, ibid.

Page 190: Rasputin, AP Images.

Page 191: Tsarskoe Selo, Steve Raymer/Corbis.

Page 192 (top): Peterhof Palace, Sergey Peterman/Shutterstock.

Page 192 (bottom): The Winter Palace, Library of Congress.

Page 193: Tsar's library at the Winter Palace, a painting by Eduard Petrovich Hau, akg-images/The Image Works.

Page 194 (top): Livadia Palace, Hana/Shutterstock.

Page 194 (bottom): Pierre Gilliard with Olga and Tatiana Romanova, Corbis.

Page 195 (top): The *Standart*, Library of Congress.

Page 195 (bottom): The imperial family, SuperStock.

Page 196 (top): Nevsky Prospect, North Wind Picture Archives.

Page 196 (bottom): Fabergé egg with red cross, the Granger Collection.

Page 197: Alexei, Corbis.

Page 198 (top): Tsar Nicholas II with Alexei at the front, 1916, the Bridgeman Art Library.

Page 198 (bottom): The imperial family in the garden at Tsarskoe Selo, 1917, Library of Congress.

Page 199: Tsar Nicholas under guard, ibid.

Page 200: The imperial family in exile, Culver Pictures.

Page 201 (top): Ipatiev House, Albert Harlingue/Roger-Viollet/The Image Works.

Page 201 (bottom): Burial ceremony, Sovfoto/Eastfoto.